Colin Dann was born in Richmond, Surrey. His interest in natural history was fostered by studying the local wildlife in Richmond Park, and wildlife success came at the age of ten, when he won a London Schools Essay Competition set by the RSPCA. His prize was a copy of *The Wind in the Willows*. For many years he worked for Collins, the publishers. It was during this period that his concern for conservation led him to write his first novel, *The Animals of Farthing Wood*, which won the Arts Council National Award for Children's Literature in 1980.

Colin has since published seven further books in his Farthing Wood/White Deer Park sequence: *In the Grip of Winter* (1981), *Fox's Feud* (1982), *The Fox Cub Bold* (1983), *The Siege of White Deer Park* (1985), *In the Path of the Storm* (1989), *Battle for the Park* (1992) and *Farthing Wood – The Adventure Begins* (1994). These stories were made into a highly successful animation series for the BBC. Other titles by him include *The Ram of Sweetriver* (1986), *The Beach Dogs* (1988), *Just Nuffin* (1989), *A Great Escape* (1990), *A Legacy of Ghosts* (1991), the City Cats trilogy, *King of the Vagabonds* (1987), *The City Cats* (1991) and *Copycat* (1997), and, most recently, *Nobody's Dog* (1999).

Journey to Freedom

By the same author:

The Animals of Farthing Wood
In the Grip of Winter
Fox's Feud
The Fox Cub Bold
The Siege of White Deer Park
The Ram of Sweetriver
King of the Vagabonds
The Beach Dogs
Just Nuffin
In the Path of the Storm
A Great Escape
The City Cats
A Legacy of Ghosts
Battle for the Park
Farthing Wood – The Adventure Begins
Copycat
Nobody's Dog

JOURNEY TO FREEDOM

HUTCHINSON
London   Sydney   Auckland   Johannesburg

First published in 1999

1 3 5 7 9 10 8 6 4 2

First published in the United Kingdom in 1999 by
Hutchinson Children's Books
Random House UK Limited
20 Vauxhall Bridge Road, London SW1V 2SA

Random House Australia (Pty) Limited
20 Alfred Street, Milsons Point, Sydney
New South Wales 2061, Australia

Random House New Zealand Limited
18 Poland Road, Glenfield
Auckland 10, New Zealand

Random House South Africa (Pty) Limited
Endulini, 5A Jubilee Road, Parktown 2193, South Africa

Random House UK Limited Reg. No. 954009

A CIP catalogue record for this book
is available from the British Library

Papers used by Random House UK Ltd are
natural, recyclable products made from wood grown
in sustainable forests.
The manufacturing processes conform to the environmental
regulations of the country of origin.

ISBN 0 09 176885 3

Phototypeset by Intype London Ltd
Printed in Great Britain by
Creative Print and Design (Wales), Ebbw Vale, Gwent

Contents

For Janet

Preface

It's always sad when a zoo fails and has to close down. It's sad for the owners who have such high hopes at the beginning. It's sad for the staff who are left without a job. Most of all, it's sad for the animals who suddenly lose their home and perhaps face the prospect of never having another one. Lingmere Zoo in the north of England was one such zoo. It had been staring closure in the face for a long time. It had never been very prosperous; it was too small, with too few exhibits to be of much interest to anyone. You could walk round it in under an hour and most people did. Lingmere relied too much on visits from holiday-makers so that, off season, it scarcely ticked over. As animals died off, they weren't replaced. Despite that, it eventually cost more to feed and look after the remainder than the zoo earned from its visitors and so it had to close.

—1—

The Animals Go

The animals were aware that their little world was changing. To begin with, suddenly there were no visitors. They were used to little throngs of people moving around the grounds and frequently stopping to stare, and although most of them ignored the people anyway the animals somehow felt uneasy when there were no visitors at all. The zoo was strangely, eerily quiet. The animals themselves made less noise.

In the lion enclosure there were just two lionesses, Lorna and Ellen. They were twins, and they had the best view of the rest of the zoo. During their habitual roaming around their paddock's perimeter they could see most of the other enclosures and their occupants, and they noticed when the first cage became empty. Then, day by day, they watched the gradual disappearance of their fellow inmates. The lucky ones were transferred to other zoos and collections where homes had been found for them, but many were less lucky. Unwanted, unfit or old animals were removed from their cages and humanely destroyed. There were no homes for these poor creatures.

Ellen was nervous. She looked across to the honey badger's enclosure, the closest to her own on one side. He and the lionesses were friends; they had been neighbours since the sisters were cubs. 'Are you still there?'

Ellen called. 'Ratel, are you still there?' She saw no movement, but she continued to call.

'He's probably asleep,' Lorna grumbled. 'You know he likes the night-time best.'

'I'll wake him up then,' said Ellen. She put her face close to the perimeter fence, opened her jaws wide and roared twice.

Lorna, who had been lying comfortably on her side, got up slowly and yawned. She watched for signs of the honey badger without much interest.

Ellen cried, 'There he is!'

The little black and white animal had run to his fence. He had a stout stocky body and a large head, and when he stretched up to grasp the wire links with his powerful foreclaws his thick hide hung loose. 'Call me?' he barked.

'Just to see you hadn't gone like the others,' Ellen explained.

'Gone? Gone where? What others?'

'The koalas, the civet, the owls and the otters . . . all disappeared. Their cages are empty,' Ellen said.

'We don't know where they've gone,' Lorna added, coming up alongside her sister.

'Oh, yes – I've missed the owls' cries,' the honey badger said. 'Are we all to go, then?'

'Who's to know?' Lorna grunted.

'And where are all the *people*?' the badger asked, puzzled.

'Why should they come if there's nothing to look at?' Lorna said shrewdly.

'Don't they want to look at you any more? You lions were always the favourites.' He wasn't at all overawed by the two huge beasts, whom he remembered from their cub days. 'The rest of us are small fry by comparison.'

No one had any answers. The honey badger dropped

back on all fours and the three animals pondered their uncertain future.

'Whatever happens, I hope *we* won't be separated,' Ellen said earnestly to Lorna. She rubbed her head against her sister's tawny shoulder. 'We'd miss you too, Ratel, if we didn't have you nearby.'

The honey badger sighed. He had been alone in his cage since his mate died. 'Always hungry, always lonely,' he muttered.

Lorna caught the first part. 'Always hungry?' she echoed with an irritable roar. 'Don't we know it? There's never enough to eat. The koalas and the others must have died of starvation.'

The next day there were more empty cages, and the day after that too. Lorna and Ellen lay on the grass in the shade of the one sickly tree in their enclosure, watching for a sign of their keeper, Joel. It was a hot day, and they had not been fed. Their stomachs rumbled repeatedly. Every so often one of them lurched to her feet and padded to a rather dirty little pond to drink, before returning to the tree and slumping down again. Joel failed to show up. Late in the afternoon they were woken from a doze by Ratel. He was in a fever of excitement.

'Lions! Lions!' he cried as he ran up and down in front of the link fence. 'The animals are being killed! We're all to be killed!' He couldn't keep still.

Lorna and Ellen were quickly on their feet. 'How do you know that? How do you know?' they roared.

'I saw the humans catching the animals in their cages,' the badger cried, 'and then – and then – pressing them down and stinging them until they were quite still and limp and – and – taking them away.'

'My, you're really jumpy,' said Lorna as the honey badger continued to run and leap about.

'We've got to get out, we've got to get out,' he growled in reply. 'We're in a trap!'

'Calm down, Ratel,' said Lorna. She was the bolder of the two sisters and wasn't easily alarmed. 'You can't be sure they were being killed. There's no cause for panic yet. If the day comes when they stop feeding us altogether, *then* we'll know we're in danger.' A mighty rumble from Ellen's stomach gave emphasis to her sister's words. 'And then woe betide any creature who strays into *our* space,' Lorna finished.

The honey badger was quieter now. He moved away to a more secluded spot, and the lions lay down again. All three animals remained alert for the feeding cart. Just before dusk, it seemed almost as an afterthought, food was brought. As usual the badger kept out of sight until the keeper had gone on his way. Then he wolfed down his provisions and hid himself again as the man returned on his round.

Joel was now the sole keeper retained at Lingmere. The zoo's business was being wound up, but Joel was trying to persuade the owners to allow Lorna and Ellen to stay until someone offered them another home. He had looked after the lionesses since they were babies and felt a strong attachment to them. Sometimes he supplemented their feed out of his own pocket. However, the chances of rehoming them were slim. Every zoo had its lion quotient and two extra lionesses were not wanted anywhere. So the sisters' days were numbered unless a new home was found for them soon.

The days flicked past and the last possible date for resettlement crept closer. All the other animals, except for the honey badger, had been disposed of. He had been promised a place elsewhere, but at the last minute there had been a change of heart. Now, regrettably, he would end his days at Lingmere. The zoo's owners had no option but to put him in the hands of the vet.

There was now almost total silence in the zoo grounds. Only the occasional roar of frustration as the lions waited for food punctured the quiet. It was evening when the vet arrived, the time of day when the badger was at his most active. He was not easily caught. Despite his size, he was a powerful animal and Joel and the vet had had a hard time blocking off the escape route to the animal's underground burrow and cornering him against the fence. The badger resorted to a favourite means of defence, and produced an overpowering odour from a special gland near his tail. The men stepped back, rocked by the incredibly potent smell. The badger scuttled away and a second chase began around the cage.

'He should know *you* by now,' the vet panted. 'Can't you do something with him?'

'He's a tricky creature,' Joel replied. 'To tell you the truth I find the lions easier than this one.' He made a dive and got the badger pinned down, but holding him was another matter. The animal was surprisingly strong and Joel needed all his protective clothing to avoid injury from the huge claws and teeth. The vet rushed forward with his hypodermic needle, ready for a hasty injection, but the badger's skin was so tough that the needle fractured. The vet swore.

'We'll have to try and get him to the lab,' he said. 'I'll need another needle.'

The two men thought they had got a firm hold on the difficult animal. They reached the path outside the cage and set off for the main building. The badger squirmed desperately. All at once he made his body twist violently inside his very loose skin and wrenched himself free from the men's grip. He dropped to the ground and ran off into some bushes inside the grounds. Dusk enveloped him and the men knew they were beaten.

'He may not go far,' said Joel. 'We can't do anything until the morning.'

The vet sighed and shrugged his shoulders. 'Is it a dangerous animal?'

'No; at least, not to people.'

'What news of the lions?'

'No one's come forward. I've written to some newspapers to see if any of the tabloids might take up the cudgels for them.'

'Good idea,' said the vet. 'Did you tell them the lions are at risk?'

'You bet,' said Joel. 'I told them Lingmere Zoo wanted the lions to be taken to a wildlife sanctuary in Africa – perhaps eventually released into the wild – rather than see two young and healthy animals destroyed, but that there were no funds available for that kind of project.'

'That should hook one of them,' the vet commented. 'Well done, Joel. If I were you, I'd follow up those letters with some phone calls. Stir up their consciences. Tell them Lorna and Ellen have only days to live!'

— 2 —

But Two Remain

Away from his enclosure with its concrete-filled trench and chicken-wire shield, the honey badger was able to tunnel his way to freedom during the night. The surrounding countryside, which was well wooded, swallowed him up. No search was mounted. The chances of finding the animal were considered to be minimal and the badger was officially regarded as lost. The lionesses called for him in vain.

'Whatever will happen to us?' Ellen asked her sister morosely. 'We're on our own here now.'

Lorna slumped against the base of the tree and stared out across the empty zoo. 'I have a feeling,' she said, 'we're going to find out very soon.'

Two days later the uneasy silence at Lingmere was abruptly broken. Joel's strategy had worked and a journalist and photographer from a national newspaper arrived to interview the keeper and the zoo owners. The lionesses were photographed looking forlorn and abandoned and their story was published the next day. It told of the plight of the lonely lions, condemned to an early death because no other zoo would offer them refuge. There was tremendous public interest. Television crews visited Lingmere and Ellen and Lorna were filmed for the evening news bulletins.

The sisters were unsettled by the sudden appearance of these eager people after so long a period of quiet. They roared nervously and their distress was there for all to see and hear on the TV screen. They became a national concern and the newspaper grabbed the opportunity and rode to their rescue, promising to undertake the transfer of the lionesses to a suitable sanctuary in Africa. No expense would be spared and, effectively, Ellen and Lorna were adopted by the paper. Joel would be retained to oversee their welfare during their journey and resettlement. It was hoped that eventually the lionesses could be prepared to fend for themselves. The ultimate goal was to release them into one of the great African game parks where they could roam free. Meanwhile their diet improved. The newspaper wanted them to look in the peak of condition whilst they were in its care.

Joel was delighted with the turn of events. He knew he couldn't have planned things better: he had saved the Lingmere lions and he was rightly proud of himself. He spent more time with Ellen and Lorna, talking to them about their future as he watched them eating or resting.

The lionesses noticed their keeper's brighter mood and they appreciated the extra rations. They felt more confident themselves.

'I don't think we have anything more to worry about,' Lorna said as she watched Joel cautiously clearing up bones and other debris from their enclosure. 'We may be alone here but we've never fed better.'

Ellen licked a paw and rubbed it over her face and whiskers. Lorna's words had reminded her of the honey badger's disappearance. 'I do wonder what happened to Ratel,' she said. 'I miss him.'

'So do I,' said Lorna. 'He was a chirpy little creature and always ready to chat.'

'Do you think we'll ever see him again?'

'How can we?' Lorna returned. '*He's* gone for good but we're not going anywhere.'

She couldn't have been more wrong, of course. Arrangements were in hand with carriers for the collection of the lions and their flight to the African continent. A sanctuary for orphaned and injured game in East Africa had given its support to the scheme. Its staff were well qualified to care for big cats and had the necessary experience for the difficult task of training them to catch and kill their own prey. The place was called Kamenza. A countdown to the day of departure began in the newspaper.

Lorna and Ellen continued innocently to enjoy the new regime. Joel, always kindly and calm, had earned their trust. He understood the sisters: how close they were, how they relied on each other's company, showing affection in so many small ways. He loved to see them lying together in the sun, one often with a paw draped over the other's back for reassurance. He really cared about their welfare and he was keen for their transfer to be carried out smoothly.

The all-important day dawned. A truck arrived containing two large crates. The lionesses first had to be immobilised with darts bearing a muscle relaxant. Then they would be tranquillised and loaded into the crates. The operation was simple enough and Joel was confident there would be no hitch. He advised the specialist vet that Ellen should be darted first as she was the more likely of the two to fret if she saw her sister disabled. The man took aim and scored a direct hit at once. Ellen yelped and leapt away, but the drug soon took effect and she fell on her side. Lorna was immediately suspicious and roared defiance. The vet reloaded his air rifle, and Lorna bounded off. The vet tried to keep her in his sights.

'Quickly,' Joel called to the carriers' men. 'While she's over there we can get Ellen outside.' With great care the limp body of Ellen was lifted and carried out of the enclosure, and she was soon safely inside one of the crates.

Lorna became frantic. With her sister removed, she was terrified of being left entirely alone. Roaring continually, she leapt around the paddock. The vet tried another shot but it was wasted. There was now a real problem, for the noise of the gun had frightened her further, and she was now in such a panic that she would be extremely difficult to hit. She leapt blindly for the branches of the single tree, which seemed to her dazed mind to be a sort of escape route, and climbed upwards.

Joel held his head in his hands. 'It won't bear her weight!' he shouted anxiously.

The vet tried desperately to load a third dart and take aim. His hands shook slightly. The branches of the tree bowed beneath Lorna's heavy body. She nearly lost her grip and tried to scramble higher still. The vet fired again and missed. The branches cracked.

'She's falling!' Joel bellowed. The men jumped clear.

From her high point, Lorna lost her balance and made one final leap to save herself as the tree's topmost branches bent and shattered. She crashed to the ground beyond the enclosure fence, landing like a domestic cat on all fours. She raced away at once, instinctively heading for the open gate of the zoo compound where the truck had entered.

For a moment or two Joel, the vet and the other men stood still, frozen to the spot by the horror of the situation. The vet broke the silence. 'Come on, Joel.

The Land-Rover! We've got to get after her before it's too late! We may be able to get close enough for one last shot.' They dashed for the vehicle, while the other men milled about uncertainly.

Lorna headed for cover, still frightened and running at full stretch. She saw a clump of trees which marked the edge of the forest. To reach them she had to cross the access road, and then a field, bordered by a low fence, in which sheep were grazing placidly in the sunshine. Lorna crossed the empty road and vaulted the fence with ease. The sheep scattered to all corners of the field as the huge beast plunged through their midst. The Land-Rover entered the field through a gate and hurtled after her. The vet leant out of one side of the vehicle, his rifle poised.

'Try to keep steady,' he shouted tensely to Joel. The Land-Rover bounced and bucked over the uneven ground as Joel wrestled with the steering-wheel. But the men were gaining on the lioness.

Lorna was tiring. She wasn't used to any kind of vigorous exercise, and fear alone kept her aching limbs moving. The noise of the car and the men's voices seemed to be right on her tail. The tree-line was so close now. Her legs toiled over the turf. If she could just . . .

'Hold tight!' the vet called, leaning far out of the side of the Land-Rover. 'I think I can get her now!' Then there was a sudden cry of warning, followed by a thud as the vehicle hit a grass tussock at thirty miles an hour and rolled over. The vet was thrown out of the side and Joel was left hanging in mid-air, still clutching the wheel. He managed to pull himself clear. Luckily his companion was merely shaken; he had only just missed being crushed by the vehicle as it rolled. The last they saw of Lorna was her tail vanishing between the trees.

*

Neither man was badly hurt. They sat on the grass for a while to recover themselves, then they righted the car. There was little damage done; it had had a soft landing.

'We're in real trouble now,' Joel muttered. 'Lorna could go anywhere. There's no vehicle access to the forest. It's very dense – impassable in places – and a lot of it's on rocky ground.'

The vet looked grim. 'The newspaper people are going to be delighted about this,' he said.

'What do we do with Ellen?' Joel asked himself aloud. 'Does she go on her own?'

'We'd better get back,' was all the vet said. 'We need to warn the police.'

Joel drove the Land-Rover back across the field a lot more hesitantly than before. They reached the zoo and were bombarded with questions by the men from the carriers. Joel and the vet explained what had happened, and the men went into the office building together to report and ask for instructions. There were long conversations on the telephone. The police arrived on the scene.

Later, a distraught Ellen, confined to her crate, roared for her sister. But Lorna couldn't hear her. She was lying exhausted on a bed of dead leaves in the thickest part of the woodland.

——3——

Lorna Alone

It was decided that Ellen would make the trip to Africa without Lorna. The transport arrangements had been made and paid for. The flight was booked. Ellen had to go. She couldn't be put back into the lions' old enclosure at Lingmere, for the zoo had closed for good. Joel was booked on the same flight, so he had to leave the hunt and attempted recapture of Lorna to others; he could play no part in that. He had to look after the handover of Ellen at Kamenza, and expected to stay in Africa for a week.

Lorna awoke in darkness with an overwhelming feeling of loneliness. For a while she lay still. She didn't remember at first where she was. But she knew she was completely alone. 'Sister! Sister!' she bellowed in her misery. Her alien roars echoed through the forest, baffling the night creatures.

There was one creature, however, who recognised the sound immediately. He had been familiar with those cries most of his life. The honey badger heard the lioness and knew that he was not the only stranger in the woodland. He stood by the entrance to the underground den he had dug for himself following his escape.

'The lions must have escaped too,' he murmured.
'But that was a cry of distress. I wonder what is
wrong.'

The roaring continued but became more distant.
The badger decided to search for his friends. 'I may
be of some comfort,' he thought. 'Company's difficult
to come by when everyone's a stranger.'

There was no answering call to Lorna's cries. Ellen was
far away. Lorna's last memory of her sister was seeing
her carried lifeless from the only home they had ever
known. The lioness was frightened, sad and thirsty. The
chase across the field had tired her dreadfully and she
longed for a drink. She padded through the gloomy
forest, fearing every moment that the men would suddenly pounce on her and shoot her down as they had
her sister. There didn't seem to be any water anywhere.
She had no real idea how to look for it, but her discomfort made her keep moving. There was almost no
sound in the woods. Layers of pine needles under the
trees deadened her steps and seemed also to muffle
the slightest noise. An occasional bird call from a high
branch was all that could be heard. There was no
breeze.

Lorna reached a clearing in the forest. On the other
side of it she at last caught the tinkling sound of
running water. She wasn't familiar with the sound, but
the scent of the water made her bound forward. A
narrow stream ran between grassy banks. Lorna
splashed eagerly into it and lapped greedily. Then she
lay on the bank in a patch of moonlight, wondering
what to do next. She fell into slumber again and was
only woken by the early morning bird chorus. She got
up, recalling at once that she was no longer in her
usual surroundings, that she was horribly alone and

that she hadn't been fed. Nor would she be fed. Lorna
had the intelligence to realise that she had run away
from her only source of food. Hunger and a feeling of
isolation made her roar again. The birds were silenced
briefly; then a medley of alarm calls rang out from a
dozen different perches in the trees.

Lorna was deaf to them. She paced along the stream
bank, her great head held low. The muscles of her
neck and shoulders rippled with each step as her tan
body passed in and out of the shadows. Scores of eyes
hidden in the foliage watched the huge animal move
along. Lorna stopped at a point where the stream
entered a narrow cave mouth. She saw that it continued
to run on into the darkness inside. The cave entrance
was well hidden by growths of bramble and fern which
trailed down across it. Lorna put her head through the
opening, blinking curiously, but ventured no further
into the interior. Then she wandered on, her stomach
rumbling constantly.

She had a dim feeling that she was taking herself
farther and farther away from the one place where
there had always been food. 'Perhaps I should go back,'
she said to herself. 'Maybe there *is* meat there still.'
She hesitated, remembering the events of yesterday.
'No,' she growled. 'I won't. Not in daylight. But when
it's dark again . . .'

She spent the rest of the day moving from one spot
to another in the thick woodland, frequently lying
down to doze. Startled pheasants and wood pigeons
clattered into the air as she disturbed them from the
ground. Other smaller birds fluttered from branch to
branch, puzzled by Lorna's intrusion. Inquisitive but
anxious, they kept her in view as her soft steps trod
through their territories.

As dusk fell Lorna was eager to begin her quest
for meat. She retraced her wanderings, guided by the

stream, and eventually reached the edge of the forest. She saw ahead of her the field where the men had nearly caught her, and sniffed the air for human scent. Was it safe to go on? It seemed to be. She padded over the turf, putting the sheep to flight by her approach. Any one of them could have been caught and killed easily, but Lorna didn't know them as meat so she ignored them and went on her way. She came to the road on the other side of which, further along, were the zoo buildings. Earlier in the day the area had been busy as plans were discussed for the lioness's recapture, but now all was in total darkness. The road was quiet. Lorna stopped on its verge, trying to detect the slightest hint of a scent of meat. And there was one! She moved in its direction.

A squirrel had been run over and the smell of the carrion had attracted the lioness. She found the carcass and sniffed at it. 'This isn't like the usual meat,' she told herself. She grasped the remains in her jaws and tugged them free from the tarmac. 'But it definitely is meat.' Back in the field she devoured all she could, leaving only scraps of fur, but her hunger was far from satisfied. She returned to the road. 'There must be more of this somewhere,' she reasoned.

Lorna sought in vain. There were no other casualties to be found. As she prowled along the road the sound of a distant car engine brought her to a halt. She tensed and listened. The growing noise reminded her at once of the Land-Rover giving chase across the field, and she turned tail and loped swiftly back to the fence she had leapt before. She hastily bounded over and ran for the safety of the woods. There were to be no further alarms that night and no further food. But as the hours passed, Lorna's hunger took precedence over every other sensation, even the feeling of loss at being parted from Ellen. So her sense of smell was heightened and constantly alert for the faintest taint of meat.

The men who were organised to trap Lorna were counting on her hunger. Her inability to hunt was their trump card. The group was composed of ex-keepers from Lingmere Zoo who were now temporarily in the pay of the interested newspaper. They were advised by a zoologist and they were on a hefty bonus for an early result. Although the area around the old zoo was scantily populated, there was still an urgent necessity to remove the threat that Lorna posed. The forest was made a no-go zone for the public. Police patrolled the perimeter roads. At various pedestrian points of entry, particularly where Lorna had first evaded Joel and the vet, traps were set using strong-smelling raw meat as bait. It was believed that the lioness would be most likely to approach at night.

Lorna hadn't forgotten the squirrel carcass. The taste of carrion hadn't left her. The next night she set off in desperation; nothing except water had passed her lips during the day. It wasn't long before she caught her first whiff of the stale meat. She quickened her pace and headed once more for the sheep pasture.

The trap here was being watched by three men, one of them an armed policeman. They were confident that it was at this spot that they had the best chance of ensnaring her. They talked in whispers and kept as still as they could. There was very little to be heard from the forest rim. An owl hooted and was answered by its mate.

Lorna's great paws scarcely disturbed the leaf litter. She stopped now and then to check the scent of the meat, drooling copiously. She was so hungry she could think of nothing but finding and gorging on the meat.

But her lion's instinct still ensured she used caution.
As she neared the lure a twig underfoot snapped. She
moved on. The waiting men tensed, holding themselves
ready, exchanging questioning glances. The heady
smell of the rancid meat drew Lorna forward. One
step, two steps . . . her head pushed through the undergrowth. She saw the meat, yet hesitated long enough
to listen. The men were breathing hard in their
excitement, and Lorna caught the sound. She growled
low in her throat, contemplating a final mad dash for
the food, and then a faint click as the policeman
cocked his weapon made her roar angrily. She knew
they were waiting for her. Frustration, fury and defeat
combined in that roar. She turned, shaking the vegetation and roaring again. The men switched on
powerful lamps which flooded the foreground in an
arc of piercing brilliance, and Lorna glanced back,
frightened by the sudden glare. The policeman raised
his gun, but Lorna crashed out of sight, plunging back
into the sheltering woodland.

'She's getting away!' one man shouted. 'Come on,
we might just catch her.'

'Not without killing her,' said the policeman. 'Should
I shoot?'

'Better not. We're supposed to take her alive unless
we're in extreme danger.'

'We can't follow her, then. Too difficult.'

The ex-keepers cursed their luck. 'Nearly had her,'
said one. 'I wonder what alerted her?'

'Oh ho, she's clever,' said the other. 'I know her of
old. She'll be a match for us.'

'She won't be back for the meat,' the police
marksman remarked grimly. 'The trick failed and she'll
have learnt from it, I'll bet.'

'She must be famished, though,' the keeper pointed
out. 'Hunger will force her to take risks in the end.'

'Well, she can't be allowed to roam free for long. People's lives are at stake. There may have to be a full-scale hunt mounted before she's much older. And we won't be keeping our fingers off the trigger then.'

Lorna loped through the forest without pausing to look back, making for the one place where she believed no one would find her: the cave where the stream disappeared. There she had her best hope of hiding herself. She reached the cave mouth and entered, splashing through the stream. The cave was narrow at the stream's inlet but opened out after a while. Lorna pulled herself on to the dry earth floor and shook her coat. She roared in exasperation, sending echoes through the darkness which startled her. The air was cold and fetid and there was a smell of something which had long rotted. Lorna began to cast about, sniffing over the floor, and found animal remains – shreds of skin and shards of bone too dessicated for even a starving lion to contemplate swallowing. But there were also fresher remnants of a carnivore's meals. Lorna devoured these gratefully, sparse as they were. She crept further into the cave's interior, completely absorbed by her quest for food. For the moment all thought of the men who had deceived her was forgotten. She found various discarded chunks of prey: heads, feet, entrails, tails, all in differing stages of decomposition. Some she gulped down, others she rejected. Finally she turned to the stream again to drink.

Where had the food come from? Lorna didn't know and didn't care. It was enough for her that it was there. She had some idea that other animals were living in the cave or had lived in it, but she didn't give that much thought either. She yearned for Ellen's company.

'Where are you, sister? Where have you gone?' Lorna

moaned to herself. 'I can't live here on my own. How cruel to separate us! I never trusted men as you did. They frighten me, but I shan't show it. If they come after me, I'll defend myself. They are deceivers, all of them!' She growled angrily and walked to the cave entrance, where she listened hard. There was no evidence that the men were on her trail. The woods sheltered Lorna in a blanket of dark and quiet. She relaxed and lay down near the water's edge.

During the night a fox caught and killed a rabbit. The rabbit screamed. Lorna heard its cry, lifted her head inquisitively, then lay down again. A short while afterwards the fox, with the rabbit clamped in its jaws, confidently entered the cave. It brought most of its victims there to eat in peace. The cave was the fox's lair.

Lorna heard the patter of the animal's claws. She sprang up, and at the same moment the fox detected her smell. It was a strange smell, quite unlike anything the fox had experienced before. The rabbit was dropped. Lorna moved towards it on her silent feet. She smelt blood and a low growl rumbled in her throat. In an instant the two hunters saw each other. The fox tried to snatch up its prey before escaping, but Lorna whipped out a paw and struck the rabbit from its grip, at the same time catching the fox such a blow that it was knocked senseless. Lorna ignored it. The rabbit was meat; the best she had had since escaping from the zoo. She tore at it greedily.

The fox wasn't dead. Lorna finished the rabbit and, only partially satisfied, moved towards the motionless body of its killer. There was blood around the fox's muzzle. Lorna growled. Could this be another, more satisfying meal? She opened her huge jaws and grasped the fox around the throat. Seconds later, Lorna had made her first kill and learnt another lesson.

—4—

Sisters Apart

Joel sat in the cabin of the cargo plane and waited for take-off. Loading Ellen had been an upsetting business for him. She was nervous and highly stressed without her sister, and Joel's familiar figure had only steadied her a little. A further mild dose of sedative had had to be administered. Now, as Joel looked out of the window at the featureless expanse of the airport, he thought of her in the aircraft hold. Ellen was being taken thousands of miles away from Lorna. How would she cope with all the changes in her life without the reassurance of Lorna by her side? The lionesses had never been parted before. To recapture Lorna alive could be a protracted operation; it would be dangerous and difficult and might result in failure. What then? The people at Kamenza would be unable to release Ellen into the wild on her own; used to captivity, she would have no chance of competing for prey without a partner. The sisters needed each other; otherwise they had no future.

It was a long flight to East Africa. There was plenty of time for Joel to think about all the problems that lay ahead, to say nothing of the major one he had left behind. He sighed deeply and tried to be optimistic. Things might work out with a generous slice of luck.

*

Ellen's low, sedated growls were drowned by the noise of the aircraft's engines. Eventually she fell silent, panting slightly with fright, but after a while she got used to the noise and the regularity of it seemed to increase her drowsiness. She couldn't believe that her solitude was permanent. She felt that her present suffering was some kind of punishment and that eventually it would end. Then, somehow, she and Lorna would resume their life together.

Ellen dozed, half awake and half dreaming, still under the influence of the tranquilliser. She dreamt of Lorna and herself, playing as youngsters in the enclosure at Lingmere. She couldn't remember her mother, but Lorna had always been there with her as they grew and matured into the powerful adults they now were. Where was Lorna now? Ellen's last memory of her sister was her threatening growls as she – Ellen – had been pierced by the human's shot. Anywhere outside the Lingmere enclosure was beyond Ellen's imagination, except for other areas of the zoo. She couldn't picture Lorna anywhere else.

'Why have they done this?' Ellen murmured sorrowfully. 'Why have they left my sister alone and tormented me like this?' She lay on her side, listening to the aircraft's drone. Her body vibrated with a sort of low hum, and she drifted into a deep sleep.

As Ellen slept during her long journey to a new land, Lorna lingered in the forest cave, her appetite for the moment satisfied. Her unplanned kill had provided sufficient meat to rid her of the hunger pangs that had been racking her since her escape. Moreover, Lorna had found a haven where she felt comparatively safe. She certainly felt less threatened.

When it began to grow light she left the cave and stood motionless by the stream, listening as always for human sounds. She had learnt caution. However, nothing could be heard that gave her concern. Numerous birds were at the stream edge, dipping their beaks into the water and throwing back their heads to savour the tiny droplets they took into their throats. Lorna was so still the birds were unaware of her presence, but when she stepped towards them, meaning no harm – she too needed to drink – they took to the air at once in a mass, chirping and screeching their alarm calls. Others who wanted to reach the water perched nearby and scolded the huge interloper. Lorna ignored them and drank her fill. Then she sat on the bank, washing her face with her paws with elaborate thoroughness. Her fur was thickly stained with the fox's blood.

Some of the bolder birds began to mob Lorna, flapping and buzzing around the mysterious animal, having no way of recognising her vast strength. They screeched at her, trying to dislodge her from the spot. For a while Lorna tolerated the mild irritation, but eventually some strayed too close. With a nonchalant flick of her mighty paw, Lorna brushed them away as if they were no more than flies. The birds crumpled instantly and dropped to the ground where they lay still. Lorna glanced at them without interest, but there was something about their appearance which struck a chord in her memory. The little bloodstained bodies were very like some of the remains she had first found in the cave and eaten eagerly.

'These might be useful later,' she told herself. 'But I could do with more of them.' She moved closer to them then and examined them. 'I'll need bigger ones in future.' Lorna was gaining in confidence. She had almost forgotten about the human threat.

The rest of the jittery birds had fluttered back to their perches in the high branches. Lorna glanced up at them, lazily watching their hurried movements. She yawned and stretched. Sunlight began to fill the forest clearing and Lorna sought the warmest corner, resting her back against the trunk of a pine and narrowing her eyes against the glare. There was no need to do anything for a while. Lorna had the typical cat's genius for saving energy until it was required.

The meat lures placed at forest entrances dried rapidly in the hot sunshine. Swarms of flies settled on them and laid their eggs. The meat had hardly been tasted by any beast and not at all by Lorna. The police officer's prediction had been correct. Yet the team assembled by the newspaper knew that Lorna was no hunter, and they wondered why hunger hadn't driven her out of hiding.

'Perhaps she's not in the woods any more,' one of the old keepers suggested. 'She could travel a long way overnight.'

'Too big not to be noticed by someone,' replied a colleague. 'No tracks anywhere, are there? No tracks at all.'

'The ground's too dry for pug marks to show up,' the first man returned. 'I still think it's possible.'

The team leader said, 'We'll have to search the forest. There's no other way. They want results. The police are fretting and the *Daily*'s scribes are running out of stories.'

'When do we go?'

'Tomorrow. Unless something brings her out before then, but I wouldn't count on it. We'll start early morning – that's the best time.'

'Will you be armed?'

'With the stun gun, yes.'

'And then what?' the sceptical man asked. 'If you

manage to hit her, how are we supposed to carry a fully grown, unconscious lion out of the woods?'

'It depends where we find her.'

'*If* we do.'

'Yes, all right, Brian,' the leader responded wearily. 'We *have* to find her some time and we must simply hope she's not buried herself too deep in there. Because there's no way we can get a trailer anywhere except on the edge of the forest.'

'Unless we clear a path?'

'It'd take too long. You can't start felling trees and expect a lion to wait around while you're doing it.'

'It sounds to me,' the sceptical Brian declared, 'as if the cards are pretty well stacked in Lorna's favour.'

The lioness had reached the point where she didn't need human help any more. She stayed near the cave during the day, sleeping and grooming herself. Birds kept their distance now, except when she was asleep. Lorna crunched up the tiny dead creatures who had strayed too close, swallowing bones, feathers and all. She wanted bigger prey. Occasionally during the day she saw a flash of movement under the trees; a squirrel or a rabbit, usually at a distance. Lorna remembered how the songbirds had been brought down, and planned to use the same method on other quarry.

At dusk, as the air cooled, she was ready for more activity. Silently and with all her senses sharp and keen, she set off to hunt. The native animals of the woodland, predator or prey, were mostly ignorant of Lorna's presence in their midst. When one or other did see the huge beast moving beneath the trees it would first scamper to a safe place and then look back with curiosity. Twice Lorna came close to catching an animal unawares. A weasel emerged from a hole in front of her nose but ducked back with astonishing speed before Lorna could strike. She sat and waited for its reappearance but the weasel knew better and Lorna eventually grew bored and went on her way. Her second chance came near a badger's sett where some young badgers were romping in the moonlight. Lorna loomed close, casting a great shadow over their antics. As she raised her massive paw the badgers sensed her presence and scampered for their tunnels. Lorna growled in annoyance and moved on.

A little later the lioness was intent on following a large animal that was browsing here and there as it explored a shrubbery. It was a solitary roe deer stepping daintily while it craned upwards to pick off some choice leaves. The deer was naturally one of the most timid and nervous of the woodland's inhabitants, and Lorna's approach had to be the essence of caution. One step at a time, keeping her head and body low, the lioness edged closer. Again and again the deer paused and held itself perfectly still as it listened, before returning to its browsing. Lorna, like all cats a mistress of stealth, had the patience to match. Little by little she neared her goal. The deer moved to a fresh growth of leaves on another plant. Lorna began to see that it was unlikely that she could get quite close enough to fell this animal with a blow. She prepared to spring.

A dry leaf rasped. The deer was startled. Lorna leapt and just caught the deer's hocks as it skittered away. The lioness's weight momentarily slowed the animal, which shrieked in fear and pain, but Lorna hadn't been able to get a firm enough grip and the deer bounded off. Lorna was left to roar her annoyance and frustration as she lay full length on the carpet of dead leaves. The thunder of her complaint rolled through the woodland, reverberating in the clear night air.

Ratel, the honey badger, heard the roar and recognised it at once. He was far closer than last time, and hastened forward, growling excitedly to himself. Night-time was his hunting time too. Voles, mice, frogs and birds had all fallen to his cunning and skill. He was an excellent climber and had taken eggs from lofty nests. But now, above all, he wanted to find his friends. He began to call. 'Lions! Lions!' he squealed noisily.

Lorna stood up and shook her head, grumbling at herself. She saw movement and swung round. A white and black animal was scampering towards her joyfully. At first she didn't recognise her old neighbour. She crouched, ready for a leap; she had learnt the lesson of her previous failure.

'I found you! I found you!' the honey badger cried in triumph.

Lorna relaxed. The animal voice she knew so well had registered just in time. 'Ratel,' she boomed in surprise. 'Do you live *here*? I – we – I thought you were dead.'

'I came close to it,' the badger answered. 'The humans wanted to kill me but I outwitted them. I escaped and I've avoided them ever since.'

Lorna was pleased. 'I'm glad you're free too. If only . . .'

'Your sister? Are you alone? Where is she?'

'I don't know,' Lorna answered sadly. 'The men shot her and she collapsed. I managed to trick them too. They've been trying to catch me but I found a – a – dark place. I hide there. I miss Ellen terribly. I don't know how to find her.'

The badger understood. 'You can't find her,' he said. 'You must learn to live alone, lion. Like me.'

Lorna sighed deeply. 'I have been learning,' she said. 'It's difficult. Will you . . . stay around here?'

'Yes, now I've found you.'

Lorna was comforted. 'I'm glad. Have you made a home?'

'Several. And there are ready-made dens all over the forest. I just move from place to place. It's simple – the creatures who made them just run away from me. I make myself fierce.' He bared his huge teeth in a sort of grin. 'They can't compete. They're a soft lot. But you must have found that out?'

Lorna considered. 'Sort of,' she admitted. 'I'm not quite used to the place yet. Oh, *you've* been gone a long time.'

'Yes, I can hardly remember the old place. I never realised there *was* all this' – he meant the world beyond the zoo – 'it's marvellous. So much space. So much to eat.'

Lorna picked up on that. 'Is there? For you? Where do you find it?'

The badger explained how he hunted. 'You can do the same,' he added, 'though you need bigger game.'

'Yes. I've seen some of it. I missed last time. I must look for more.' A thought struck Lorna. 'How did you find me?'

'I heard you calling for your sister – I've been searching ever since. And then I heard you roaring tonight.'

'Ratel, you're my friend. And I'm yours.'

'Of course. As always. Are you hungry, lion?'

'I certainly am.'

'Come with me,' said the honey badger. 'I'll dig some meat up for you.' He trotted away, the huge lioness padding behind him. They came to a burrow with several entrances. 'This is where they vanish when they think they're in danger,' the badger explained. He ripped at the soft dry soil with his powerful claws. In no time he had torn his way into the tunnel system. The speed with which he dug into the earth and flung it behind him astonished even Lorna. Two rabbits dashed out of the warren in panic. Lorna crushed one with a blow. Her companion seized the other in his teeth. Lorna roared her approval.

'Don't stand a chance, do they?' Ratel chirruped with his jaws full. 'It's so easy.'

Lorna appreciated the unexpected meal. 'I'm grateful,' she said. 'Soon I hope to surprise *you*.' She was proud and wanted to rely on herself. 'Stealth is the key. Stealth and strength.'

——5——

Supremacy

Lorna was not alone in employing stealth. The men who comprised the search party early next morning were every bit as furtive. They trod carefully and hardly spoke as they entered the forest from the sheep field, carrying nets, rope and a sling. At each step they searched for a clue that Lorna had passed that way; that they were on her trail. However, they were not experienced trackers, so only the more conspicuous signs left by the lioness were likely to be noticed. They penetrated deep into the woodland, feeling less like watchers than the watched. The men were tense and anxious, aware that at any moment the elusive Lorna might suddenly crash through the undergrowth alongside them. They kept close together.

The team leader, Martin, tried to instil some confidence into the party. 'There's nothing to worry about. If she hears or sees us she's going to run from us. *That's* when we have to be on our toes if we're to catch her.'

'But we can only pursue her if you've managed to dart her,' Brian remarked. 'What if you miss?'

'We carry on trailing her and try again. She's more frightened of us than we are of her.'

One of the others murmured, 'Want a bet?'

They kept on steadily. At last they found some evidence that they recognised in the shape of fairly fresh dung. 'Unmistakable,' said Martin. 'Good. She's still around.'

'It's a big forest,' another man remarked cynically. He had just spoken when the search party stopped abruptly, each man glued to his spot. A low growl in the near distance had been heard by all of them.

'That's her.' Martin spoke with assurance. 'Now's our chance. Proceed with caution.'

'What were we using before?' the cynic whispered with a smothered laugh.

They saw a slight disturbance in the midst of a growth of fern about twenty metres ahead. They crept forward slowly, without any sound. Martin held his air rifle ready. Lorna's tawny coat was clearly visible amongst some greenery. As the men approached she emerged from the ferns, rear end first, dragging something backwards. She had no suspicion of the men's proximity, absorbed as she was with hauling a young deer she had killed free of the vegetation. She dropped her kill to get a better grip. One of the men gasped, partly in surprise, partly in admiration. He couldn't restrain himself, and Lorna heard him. She spun round, saw the men, and, pausing only to snatch her prey in her great jaws, lumbered away, lugging the carcass between her forelegs.

Martin took a sight and pressed the trigger but Lorna's lurching movement caused the dart to go over her head. Now the men ran forward, Martin leading.

'Get the nets ready!' he cried. 'If we can entangle her, I'll shoot again.'

Lorna was encumbered by the deer and the men were pressing her. She hated to lose her kill, but her fear overcame her appetite. She discarded the carcass and jumped into some dense brushwood, burrowing away out of sight until she could pull herself clear on the other side. Then she raced for her den, instinctively heading for the darkness of the cave. The men were thwarted for the moment.

For a while longer the team persisted, following the direction of Lorna's flight and expecting every minute to find her skulking in the undergrowth. But there was no trace of her. They searched other tracts of the woodland but drew a blank in each one of them. Reluctantly Martin decided to abandon the hunt for that day.

'She's bound to leave the forest now,' said Brian. 'She knows it's not safe.'

Martin pursed his lips. 'We'll see,' he said phlegmatically. But he was worried.

During the night Lorna retrieved her kill. She ate her fill while the honey badger watched her enviously. He was permitted to polish off her leavings and this set the pattern for the future.

Far from feeling insecure, as some of the men thought, Lorna believed herself to be completely safe. She had the perfect lair in her cave. The men hadn't followed her there which seemed to prove to Lorna that, as long as she had her secret bolt-hole, she could come and go as she liked. The deer meat had thoroughly satisfied her and she wouldn't need to kill again for a while. Also, the appearance of the honey badger had ended her isolation. For the time being she was content. Memories of Ellen still hovered in her mind but they were slowly fading. The increased activity of life in the woodland occupied Lorna in a way she had never known before.

The honey badger took to following her around. He had spent most of his life alone – first in the zoo and then in the woods – and he relished having a companion. Lorna tolerated his presence up to a point. She enjoyed the familiarity of her old friend but there

were times when she wanted to be on her own. She
soon made this apparent.

'Now, Ratel, where is your den?' she asked pointedly
as the badger showed signs of wanting to join her in
the cave. She stood by the entrance, blocking the hole
with her body and watching him lazily.

'Oh, anywhere convenient,' he replied airily. 'I'm
not fussy so long as it's dark and hidden away.'

'Don't you have a special place?'

'No-o, not really. I just—'

'Well,' Lorna interrupted him, 'this is my special
place and mine alone. And I want to keep it that way.
You understand me, don't you?'

The badger backed slightly. Lorna was so huge and
imposing. 'Er – yes. Yes, I understand.'

'Even humans keep away from here,' Lorna continued, 'so, you see, it's a sort of secret place.' She
yawned and stretched her mighty limbs. 'Of course,
I'm happy to have you nearby, you know.'

'Nearby. Yes,' the badger echoed. The position was
clear enough and he accepted it. He lifted a back leg
and scratched his belly. He wasn't afraid of Lorna but
he was aware of her strength and respected it. 'I'll leave
you, then, lion,' he said and trotted away. He turned
once to look at her majestic figure and paused in
admiration. 'There's nothing to rival her here,' he
murmured.

Lorna already felt her position of supremacy in the
forest. Her stature gave her a new assurance. At times
she heard human voices, but as her knowledge of the
woodland grew she found it easy to evade any attempt
to recapture her. The men were frustrated at every turn
and realised they needed new tactics. It was decided to
use dogs for the first time to try to flush Lorna from

cover. In that way the men hoped to have just time enough to dart and sedate her.

Lorna had no experience of dogs and the men knew that. 'She won't know how to deal with them,' Martin said. 'They'll confuse her. It'll be our best chance yet. She's become too wary. Even the police helicopter couldn't pinpoint her. But the dogs'll make a difference.'

A working bloodhound with its handler was hired. The dog was introduced to Lorna's scent at the zoo and set on her trail. The men followed with a pair of bull mastiffs which were to be used to keep the lioness at bay. These dogs were utterly fearless but, just as Lorna had no knowledge of dogs, so the dogs had never seen a lion.

By now Lorna's range in the forest was extensive. She knew the best places to stalk deer and where the rabbit runs were. Twice more she had encountered and killed foxes. She had learnt always to listen for unusual sounds in the daytime. She knew that humans preferred the daylight hours. On the morning when Martin led his team of men and dogs into the forest by the usual route, Lorna was in her lair. But she wasn't sleeping. An overpowering thirst kept her wakeful and she returned continually to the stream to drink. The bloodhound picked up her scent very quickly and bayed deeply. Lorna raised her head. It was a sound she didn't recognise. But she knew it was an animal sound and, to Lorna, an animal sound in these woods meant possible prey.

She was alert and curious at once. She left the cave, intent on investigating. Silent as ever, she travelled beneath the trees. The men were not so silent. They had given the bloodhound its head and were now hurrying to keep up with it. The bull mastiffs trotted at

the men's side. Lorna soon detected the men's hasty
steps and took her customary evasive action. She set
forth on a wide detour, taking her to the fringe of the
woodland and bringing her round to the men's rear.
The loud snuffling of the bull mastiffs, who breathed
badly, intrigued Lorna and she followed in their wake.

Meanwhile the bloodhound was becoming confused.
Lorna's scent was everywhere in the forest. The hound
tried to keep its nose to the freshest trail but the lioness's tracks were a sort of maze. They diverged here,
met up again there, dividing and rejoining constantly.
Finally the hound found the most recent scent and
barked in excitement. It bounded along then on the
very route Lorna had taken that morning. The men
were outdistanced and found it difficult to keep the
bloodhound in view. Lorna, however, was ready for it.

She heard the dog's triumphant bark and took cover.
Shortly   afterwards   she   saw   the   bloodhound
approaching. To Lorna the animal resembled nothing
she had ever seen before, except that there was some
slight similarity in the way it moved to that of a fox.
Lorna knew all about foxes. She crouched behind her
screen of undergrowth, preparing to pounce.

The bloodhound's head was up as the lioness sprang
but the dog never knew what hit it. Lorna's crushing
weight drove the breath from its body and her jaws
fastened on its throat. But she didn't have time to
carry off her kill. The men were approaching. Lorna
hesitated, then dropped the carcass and loped quietly
away unseen, snarling to herself in exasperation.

The dog-handler was the first on the scene. 'My God,
Martin! Look at this!'

The rest of the men trudged up, breathing heavily.
The handler was on his knees, examining the remains
of the unfortunate bloodhound. The bull mastiffs
sniffed at the carcass with puzzled expressions.

Martin looked strained. 'This is awful,' he said. Then, angrily, 'She's not to get away with this! She can't be far. Come on, lads. Let's go after her.'

None of the others was keen. 'I can't leave Bruno like this,' the dog-handler said, looking sadly at the bloodhound. 'I have to take him back.'

'Yes. Yes, I'm sorry. This is a tragedy,' said Martin. 'We'll help. You can use the sling to carry him. Brian, Dean, will you help? Take Bruno to the car. Then come back and join the rest of us.' He wiped a hand wearily over his face. 'I can't say how sorry I am about all this. It's just . . . unbelievable.'

'It's a cruel waste,' said the dog-handler. 'Bruno couldn't have stood a chance.' He shook his head. The bloodhound's body was lifted on to the sling. 'The mastiffs are no good to you now,' he said. 'They're not tracking dogs.'

'I'd like to keep them a bit if we may,' the leader replied. 'They make us feel less vulnerable.'

The handler nodded. 'As you like, but keep them on their leads. We don't want any more accidents. If you come up with the beast, they'll play their part. But I wouldn't think you stand much chance now.' He turned to go.

'Where will you be, boss?' Brian asked as he and Dean lifted their burden, grunting with the weight. 'Where will we find you?'

'Round about here. If Lorna has left this area we'll call it a day. But *I* think she's lurking nearby. She'll be thinking about her—' He broke off. He'd been about to say 'kill' but it was too sensitive a word while the dog-handler was still within earshot. 'You know what I mean,' he finished in an undertone.

The three men departed. Those remaining had lost heart. The lioness was too clever for them, too strong and too savage. She had everything in her favour and they weren't happy about that. But Martin was determined to continue. Beset by constant failure and reversals, and under increasing pressure from their employers on the national newspaper, the team needed somehow to justify themselves. Martin knew it and wouldn't give up. Besides, he was furious at being outwitted once again.

Lorna was lying up in some bracken, well hidden, but still in the vicinity. Martin had been right: she hadn't forgotten her abandoned meal. The men, with very little enthusiasm, began their search. All of them, Martin included, had the same uncomfortable feeling of being watched. The bull mastiffs felt the men's tension and stiffened visibly. Lorna was supremely quiet and still. She could see the human figures in the near distance. They never came very close.

Eventually Brian and Dean rejoined the group. All the men wanted to quit the forest. They had had nothing but bad luck in it, and didn't think they had the remotest chance of any success.

'We're not achieving anything here,' one complained. 'Let's leave. It's an impossible job.'

There were murmurings of assent.

'You want her to beat us?' Martin said accusingly. 'One wretched animal against eight men?'

'She's not just any animal,' Dean reminded him. 'There's no shame in it, boss. We've done our best.'

'No.' Martin shook his head. 'We haven't. And that's what I'm being told. We've got to get a result here. If not today, then soon. Otherwise it'll be peanuts for all of us for all our efforts. There'll be no real pay-out.'

'What do you suggest then?' one of the other men asked.

'I've got one more idea for today,' Martin answered. 'A lion doesn't like to leave its kill. She's waiting for us to go. She'll be bound to come looking for that poor brute of a dog once she thinks it's safe to do so. Let's play her game. Get into hiding and wait.'

'Wouldn't she know we're still around?' Brian asked. 'She could scent us, surely?'

'Not if we're a little way away. Lions rely more on their eyes and ears than their noses. But we must be completely quiet. Including the dogs. Shall we give it a chance?'

There were half-hearted responses.

'How long do we wait?'

'As long as it takes.'

'But what if she doesn't come back?'

'She will,' said Martin. 'I know it.'

'Then why didn't we try this idea before? When we nearly had her at the deer kill?'

'We didn't have the dogs with us then, did we? Trackers or not, the mastiffs make *me* feel happier. We only had ourselves to rely on before.'

There was no further conversation. Martin placed his team so that they were close enough to have a good view of the scene of the kill, while at the same time being sufficiently well hidden to be not immediately noticeable. There was nothing to do then but wait. Not a word was exchanged. As an added precaution the bull mastiffs were muzzled. Men and dogs crouched together, watching the spot where the hound's spilt blood coagulated and began to turn solid.

Lorna was the essence of patience. She lay still for a long time. Then, growling low in her throat, as though reasoning with herself, she eventually got to her feet. She looked for signs of humans and listened for their sounds. There were none. Satisfied, she began to approach the pool of blood at a leisurely pace. The smell of it was strong and sweet. She headed directly

for it – then suddenly stopped, baffled by the disappearance of the carcass. Her angry growl was distinctly
heard by the watching men. Lorna looked ahead,
assessing the turn of events. Martin raised his rifle.
Lorna spied the slight movement and, with an astonishing burst of speed, raced towards the ambush. The
men had no time to unmuzzle the dogs who were
struggling to their feet, straining furiously, as Lorna
charged. Martin tried to hold steady but his hands
trembled. Some of the men broke away. The lioness
was almost on them.

Lorna sprang at the man with the gun, dashing it
from his hands as she vaulted over his body and
careered onwards through the undergrowth. Martin
was completely unhurt but badly shaken. Lorna had
had no intention of attacking him. It seemed she
had recognised the threat of the rifle and had deliberately planned her leap to upset it. In no time she was
once again lost from view. Some of the men were
gasping at the abruptness of Lorna's run. Others shook
their heads slowly.

'It's uncanny,' said Dean. 'She seems to *know*, doesn't
she? As though she can read our minds.'

Martin slumped on the ground, white-faced. The
men glanced at him awkwardly. One of them tried to
stir him.

'What's next, boss?'

There was no answer at first. Then Martin slowly got
to his feet. 'Resignation,' he murmured.

Into Africa

The cargo plane carrying Ellen and Joel touched down at the East African airport in late afternoon, but their journey was not yet over. There were still some miles to go by road before they reached Kamenza. Ellen's crate was unloaded and transferred to an open-top truck, and she was given fresh water and food. Tired after her ordeal, she drank all the water but barely touched the food.

Joel also was tired. Having made certain Ellen was as comfortable as possible he took the passenger seat in the car that was to follow the truck. Photographs were taken to accompany a short article in the sponsoring newspaper which would report Ellen's safe arrival on the African continent. Then the next stage of the journey began.

Ellen roused a little once on the move again. She was immediately aware of new sensations, the most noticeable of which was the heat. She had never experienced temperatures of this kind, any more than had Joel. The air was heavy and full of strange and pungent smells. Nothing remembered from her enclosure at Lingmere Zoo in the north of England was remotely akin to any of these things. Ellen was totally unprepared for the change. And yet, deep within her unconscious self, an ancient instinct was stirred and an ancestral echo reawakened.

Joel felt no such echo. The car was hot, and he was sleepy and uncomfortable. Nevertheless, he was able to marvel at the unfamiliar landscape while he wrestled with the rich accent of his friendly African driver. The truck trundled ahead and eventually turned off the metalled road, throwing up quantities of reddish dust. They passed a village where they received some enthusiastic waves. Joel waved back and grinned broadly.

'Kamenza village,' the driver announced.

'Oh yes?' said Joel. 'Then we're close?'

'We're here,' the driver replied. 'OK?'

The truck pulled into a yard. Some people came out of a building on one side and ran over to lend a hand. The car drew up in front of a house with a veranda and a short flight of steps running down to ground level. A man in shirt and shorts hastened down them as Joel got out of the car. He was the chief game warden of the nearby national park, and was also in charge of the animal refuge centre. His voice rang out.

'Joel? Simon Obagwe.' He thrust out a hand and grasped Joel's. 'Good trip?'

'Good, but long.'

'Of course. You must be worn out.' Simon smiled at the driver who was carrying Joel's luggage. 'Thank you, Paul.' He turned to Joel again. 'You'll want to freshen up and change your clothes. Come along in. Hot, isn't it?'

'Very,' Joel agreed. 'Er – I'd really like to see Ellen settled first, if that's all right.'

'Plenty of time for that. They won't do more than unload the truck until we're ready. I expect you could use some refreshment?'

Ellen sensed several sets of eyes on her as her crate was brought to the ground. She was quite used to being

stared at, but when Lorna had been with her she had
known that the attention was shared. Now she was the
sole focus of interest. She glared suspiciously at these
men with their excited chatter. She felt deserted and
vulnerable. If only her sister were with her now! She
showed her teeth in a half-snarl as one man came
particularly close to examine her.

'Beautiful, beautiful,' the man was murmuring.

Later Ellen was introduced to her roomy new pen. It
had plenty of shade and there were clear areas under
the trees where she could lie. There was also a pool.
Ellen was the only occupant. Surrounding the
enclosure was a three-metre-high wire fence with over-
hangs to prevent climbing out and a second, lower
fence around that. Support poles were sunk into con-
crete so that digging a way out wasn't an option either.
Joel noticed the emphasis on security, comparing it
with Lingmere. For the hundredth time he wondered
whether Lorna had been recaptured. He meant to find
out as soon as he could make contact with England.

'What d'you think?' asked Simon.

'I think she's very lucky,' Joel answered. 'Except she'll
be lonely. She's *always* lived with her twin before.'

'I know. An unfortunate business, that. I hope she
won't be alone for long.'

'So do I. I don't know what's happened at home.
Perhaps I could—'

'We'll find out,' Simon said promptly. 'Meanwhile
Ellen has a neighbour she can see: Upesi, a young
cheetah. We brought her in as an orphan. Her mother
injured a leg. Couldn't hunt. Starved to death, I
expect.'

Joel registered this information, given so baldly. Life
in the African wild was another cup of tea altogether.
It could be nasty and short. If Ellen – and Lorna – ever

reached the release stage, they would face a host of dangers and difficulties neither of them knew existed. How would they cope? He watched Ellen begin a cautious exploration of the pen. Release seemed a distant prospect. But at least the lioness had a chance now to become familiar with the kind of terrain she might one day roam. Her enclosure's fencing had been erected around existing vegetation, a chunk of the savannah. Ellen brushed against it, close to where Joel was standing. He spoke to her.

'It'll be all right; you'll see,' he said softly. 'You'll be well cared for. And I'll be here for a while.'

Ellen recognised his voice. She paused. Their eyes met. Joel thought he saw a kind of appeal in Ellen's gaze. He wondered whether he was imagining it. But he answered anyway. 'She's coming,' he whispered. 'Soon.' He hoped he was speaking the truth.

By now Lorna was exulting in her freedom. She had become scornful of humans and their feeble endeavours in the forest. She and the honey badger hunted throughout the woodland and they met no rivals.

One evening after filling their bellies the two animals lay by the stream. They were entirely confident in their surroundings.

'Have you ever thought,' Lorna asked lazily, 'of going beyond the forest?'

'No,' the badger answered at once. 'I don't need to. I have everything I want right here.'

'Aren't you just a little curious?'

'Not me, no. Why should I be? *This* is my territory.'

Lorna stared at him with a hint of contempt. 'Don't you want to enlarge it?'

The badger sat up. 'What's on your mind, lion?'

'I'll tell you,' Lorna answered. 'Bigger prey! I remember some creatures I saw soon after my escape.

I didn't understand about hunting then. They're still there, beyond the trees; you can hear them making their weak, silly cries. They're fat, Ratel. Very fat. I think they'd be easy game.'

'The humans are out there,' the badger protested. 'You're safer in here now they leave you alone.'

'Humans!' Lorna scoffed. 'They don't know what I'm thinking! They wouldn't be expecting me. And, besides, they shut themselves in their dens at night. I'd have a clear field. Why don't you come too? See the sport. Don't you always follow me?'

'Mostly,' the badger replied. He had no real desire to be part of Lorna's plan. 'When is this to be?'

'When I need a kill.'

Ratel considered. 'All right,' he said. 'You go first. If it goes well, I'll come the next time.'

Lorna said disdainfully, 'Of course it will go well. But I don't require your help, so you must do as you please.'

Lorna was keen to test herself. Even before hunger really asserted itself again, she was ready for the prowl. The honey badger followed as far as the woodland's rim. Lorna aimed for the sheep field she remembered so vividly, and hesitated on the edge of the trees.

'Is anything there?' the badger asked.

'I don't hear them,' Lorna growled. 'Maybe they've moved.'

'Try another time,' the smaller animal suggested.

'Nonsense. They're out there somewhere. And I'm going to find them,' Lorna finished positively.

'Be careful, lion. I want you to come back.'

Lorna's ears cocked but she didn't answer. She crept into the empty field. In her mind's eye she could see the mass of plump, top-heavy bodies that had scattered as she ran between them. Where were those funny long faces and dainty feet? She raised herself and walked more boldly across the pasture. A spectral barn owl dived earthwards and scooped up a vole. Nothing else moved.

Lorna paced her way into an adjoining field. And then she heard them. A stray bleat answered by another: a ewe calling its lamb. The lioness hastened towards the sound. White, woolly-coated bodies dotted the far side of the field. Most of the sheep were lying down, chewing incessantly. Some grazed the turf. Lorna picked out a young lamb adrift from the main flock. She sank to her belly and crawled forward, her head straight and still, her eyes fixed unwaveringly on her target. The flock had no reason to be particularly cautious. They had no history of being hunted. Lorna's progress was easy; the lamb still had its back to her when she made her final dash. It was dead before it could even bleat.

Now the flock saw the killer and panicked. But Lorna merely lugged the lamb away towards the forest, carrying it comfortably in her jaws. She ignored the rest of the sheep then, but the ease with which she had made her kill remained in her memory.

The badger was waiting for her. He had never seen a sheep and at first was puzzled by Lorna's burden.

'Did you go all that way simply for some fresh bedding for your den?' he asked in astonishment as his eyes picked out the drooping fleece.

Lorna loosened her hold for a moment. 'Very comical,' she grunted. 'In that case you won't be wanting a share?'

Now the badger saw his mistake. 'Oh. You have meat too! It smells rich.' He sniffed eagerly. 'You're very resourceful, lion. Was there any danger?'

'None at all.' Lorna grabbed the lamb again and moved beneath the trees. 'Plenty there for a determined hunter.' She reached a favourite place in some brushwood and dropped her prey. A slight warning growl kept the badger at a distance. She ripped at the thick fleece. The badger turned a somersault, unable to keep still.

'This is good meat, Ratel,' Lorna told him, turning her reddened face in his direction. 'The best. Better than the meat the men used to give us.'

Ratel swallowed. He yearned to taste it. 'Will there be . . . a mouthful or two, d'you think, lion? Just a morsel, perhaps?'

Lorna yanked another limb off the carcass. 'What I don't eat now,' she told him, 'I shall carry back to my den. This is too good to leave to the scavengers. But you can come afterwards for scraps. As you usually do.'

The badger was disappointed. He had hoped for something more this time. 'If I . . . came hunting with you – you know, *outside* – would I perhaps earn the right to a bigger portion?'

Lorna didn't reply at once. Eating took precedence. When she was satisfied she said, 'You have the right to the whole animal.' The badger grinned, showing his huge teeth. 'As long as you killed it,' the lioness added pointedly.

The badger shook his loose coat irritably. 'How could I even—'

But Lorna interrupted him. 'They have no defence,' she said. 'None. A hunter such as you would be more than a match for the smaller ones. This creature didn't even run.'

'Do they . . . do they just stand and wait to be slaughtered?' cried Ratel. His eyes glowed greedily.

'This one did. But in any case they have no speed. You wish you'd come with me this time, don't you?'

'I do regret it. And you say there are no humans to protect them?'

'As you see,' Lorna purred. 'Just as in the forest. We go where we please.'

The badger looked pensive. He couldn't quite believe that men hadn't a trick up their sleeve somewhere.

— 7 —

Hunter

The news of the failed attempts to recapture Lorna greatly disheartened her former keeper. Joel was torn between a desire to return to England to lend his special knowledge to this task and a feeling that he should remain longer at Kamenza to help care for Ellen. He was amazed by the swiftness with which Lorna had taught herself to hunt, and concluded that this had been born out of desperation.

Simon could see Joel was ill at ease. 'Don't worry,' he told the Englishman. 'It's out of your hands as long as you're here. How long you stay with us is entirely up to you.'

'Thanks,' said Joel. 'I don't like to leave Ellen while she's off her feed.'

'That won't last,' Simon assured him with a smile. 'It's all new and strange at the moment. Once she's got her bearings a bit she'll be fine.'

But she wasn't. She ate nothing at all on the first day. Simon shrugged it off. The next day Joel tried to tempt her with some fresh meat. Ellen showed scant interest. She listened obediently to his coaxing and then turned her back and wandered away. Most of the day she spent lying under the trees.

Joel was upset. 'This doesn't look good,' he said.

'It takes some animals longer to settle than others,'

Simon reassured him. 'No cause for concern yet. Ellen's
basically a fit and healthy beast. That'll tell in the long
run. Nature will take its course.'

On the third day Ellen spent most of the time at the
far end of her pen. She had discovered her neighbour
Upesi, the cheetah, and seemed to be comforted by
her presence. She lay by the wire in a patch of shade
and watched the smaller cat pacing up and down.
Occasionally the cheetah glanced in her direction.

'This is a strange place,' said Ellen.

Upesi continued to pace. 'What's strange about it?'

Ellen didn't know how to describe her feelings.
Instead she asked, 'How long have you lived here?'

Upesi was puzzled. She didn't remember her mother
and she had no way of knowing that there was anywhere
else to live. 'I'm still young,' was her answer.

'Yes, but is this your home?'

'Of course it is. What do you mean?' Now she
stopped and faced Ellen.

'I wondered if you came from somewhere else, like
me,' the lioness said.

'How could I? I saw you arrive.'

'Well, this isn't my home,' Ellen growled. 'My home's
quite different. I don't know why I'm here.' She looked
away into the distance as though trying to locate Lingmere beyond the African plain. That brought Lorna
into her mind. 'I have a sister who should be with me.
We always live together. I don't know why they parted
us.' She looked at Upesi mournfully. 'I *could* make this
place home if she were here with me.'

Upesi didn't understand. 'The man who feeds you
spends a lot of time with you,' she commented. 'I
wouldn't like that.'

'I'm used to him,' Ellen said. 'He's part of my home
too. I feel strange here and unhappy. And yet some of
it seems right. I don't know what's happening.'

'Neither do I,' said the cheetah. 'Why do you keep talking all the time?' She walked away. Her long elastic limbs moved economically. They had never yet known the explosion of speed of which they were capable.

Ellen was still trying to make some sense of the situation. 'I was at home, then I went to sleep,' she muttered to herself. 'A long sleep. Then I was in The Box. Still half asleep. A lot of noise, thunder, rumblings. Always The Box. Hoisted up. Then down again. Up and down. Then here. Out of The Box at last. Alone. All the time alone,' she finished morosely. 'But why?'

The sun had moved round. It was glaringly hot. Joel was placing a large container of milk under a bush, and Ellen went to investigate. With some persuasion she managed to lap at it. The milk was refreshing.

'That'll do you some good, anyway,' said Joel. 'But I wish you'd look at the meat.'

Ellen licked her lips. She gazed at the keeper. Her eyes glinted gold. Joel remembered that expression of appeal. He realised then that Ellen would never recover until she was reunited with her sister.

Day by day Lorna grew stronger, bolder. She returned to the sheep pasture with the honey badger trotting behind her, excited but nervous. He had never lost his distrust of humans.

The night was quiet, but Lorna paused before leaving the cover of the forest. She turned to check on her companion.

'I'm right behind you,' said the badger. 'You smell very strong. I hope the wind is in our favour – we don't want to alarm the fluffy creatures just yet.'

'Can't you smell their fat bodies?' Lorna cried.

'Er – no. Your scent tends to drown almost everything else,' the badger replied. 'I'm not complaining. It makes me braver.'

The lioness ignored his comments. 'Come on, let's hunt!'

In her habitually stealthy way she stole across the field, Ratel keeping directly behind. 'Spoilt for choice,' Lorna growled with satisfaction as she saw the flock spread out before her, innocently nibbling at the grass. She turned to the badger. 'Now, my friend, pick your prey.'

'Anything. Any one, I'll go with you.'

'All right. Let's – just – creep – a little closer. Now!'

Lorna had selected her victim, this time a fully grown ewe that she noticed moved with a limp. She broke into a run, gaining speed all the while. The badger dropped behind and finally stopped dead to watch the flock flee in every direction. Lorna wasn't distracted. She stuck resolutely to her intended target, pouncing and hanging on until the lame ewe's breaths ceased. The badger marvelled at her efficiency, and was suddenly reminded he was supposed to be hunting as well.

Some chubby lambs were trying to screen themselves behind their mothers, and the badger trotted forward purposefully, selecting the fattest and keeping after it, dogging it unswervingly as it skittered about bleating in fright. The badger's great teeth closed on a woolly hind leg. The lamb broke free, but it was maimed. It hobbled hopelessly after its mother, begging for protection. The ewe half turned and made a courageous run towards the badger, but she was easily outmanoeuvred and the plump lamb was caught. The badger began to tug it away, occasionally dropping it to avoid another fruitless rush from its mother, then taking it up again. In this way he gradually dragged the lamb back to the tree cover.

Lorna was already carrying her prize to one of her favourite spots. She hadn't seen the badger's kill. The fierce little predator, panting heavily from his labour, dragged his trophy to the same place. There was enough meat to supply him for days.

'You were successful,' said Lorna coolly. 'Good. Easy pickings, eh?'

The badger had been hoping for a little more recognition of his efforts. The lamb was a lot bigger than its killer and the badger felt that, for his size, he had performed a really prodigious feat. 'Not quite so easy for a small animal,' he gasped. 'We're not all giants.'

Lorna was tearing out tufts of wool with her teeth and paid no further attention.

These latest killings did not, of course, go unnoticed. The sheep farmer set a guard on his flock at night. He had no proof of the killer's identity but he suspected the escaped lion. He was determined to find the necessary evidence, believing Lorna had become a dangerous threat to livestock. In his view if she wasn't captured soon she should be shot.

There wasn't a lot of evidence so far; only some bloodstained ground and a few scattered strands of wool. Lorna always carried the remains of her prey, after her first meal, into the cave. As for the badger, he took what he wanted off the lamb he had killed and left Lorna to dispose of the rest. The farmer guessed the hunter would return. He tethered his dogs nearer the flock. He knew no intruder would escape the dogs' notice and that they would soon rouse their master. In that event he relied on his shotgun to scare the killer away.

Some days passed without incident. Then Lorna was ready for another raid. She began to call for her friend. It was dusk and the badger usually came trotting along when he heard the lion's rumblings, but on this occasion he didn't show up. Lorna was unconcerned. She was quite happy to hunt on her own. She went on her way, still expecting Ratel to appear at some point. She knew where his favourite burrow was, and gave a final call as she passed nearby. There was no response. Lorna accepted that she was on her own.

Further along she heard the badger's unmistakable squeal. At first she couldn't locate the sound. She heard it again and looked around irritably. 'No use calling *me*,' she growled. 'You didn't come when *I* called. If you want to join me, you know where I'm going. Catch me up.'

'Lion!' The badger's chirrup was louder. 'I'm up here!'

Lorna raised her head and saw movement in one of the tall trees. The badger was busy clawing at something among the branches. There was a tearing sound and suddenly insects were darting all round his head and body, drowning his chirps and whistles with their ferocious buzzing. The badger ignored them and continued to break open their nest. He had discovered a swarm of bees that had made their home in a tree hollow, and knew instinctively that there was honey to be had from the nest; something that was quite irresistible. There were thousands of bees in the hollow and they instantly launched an attack on the animal, but the badger's extraordinarily thick hide was impervious to the insects' stings. As he munched on the delicious sweet food, his powerful scent gland got to work, and the bees seemed to become confused. They ceased to attack and crawled all over the tree's branches and the badger's body, offering no further resistance.

Lorna watched in bewilderment. She couldn't understand what was going on. She knew the badger could climb but he was so high up in the tree that he was almost obscured by its foliage. She sat down, expecting him to fall. There was a mild thud. Something had fallen, but certainly not the badger. Lorna sniffed at

the object on the ground; it was a section of the bees'
honeycomb, with many of the bees still attached. Once
away from the honey badger's stupefying odour, they
began to function again. Stings at the ready, they auto-
matically returned to the defence of their plundered
nest. Lorna's nose was judged to be the enemy.

The honey badger's blissful enjoyment of his sticky
meal was interrupted by a heartrending roar. Startled,
he peered down through the mass of leaves, almost
overbalancing. Lorna seemed to be spinning on the
spot. Scores of bees had fastened themselves on her,
stinging her face, her legs, her shoulders. She whirled
about, maddened by the pain, one forepaw then the
other swatting in vain at her tormentors. And all
the time she roared in protest, in surprise, in agony.
In the end in sheer desperation she charged away
through the trees, heading for the only place where
she thought she might obtain relief: the stream. Slowly
the badger lowered himself down the tree-trunk, his
great claws digging deep into the bark as he went. He
was curious. Quickly demolishing the lump of honeycomb on the ground, he trotted off to find the lioness.

Lorna raced pell-mell for the water, her tawny coat
decorated with dead and dying bees. Others still followed her as though drawn by a magnet. She crashed
through the undergrowth. Brambles, briars and thorns
tore at her limbs but Lorna hardly felt them amid the
overriding pain of the bee-stings. At last she neared
the stream. Taking an almighty leap, she hurled herself
into it and pressed herself to its narrow bed. The cold
water rippled over her back and Lorna dipped her sore
head under the surface. The last of the bees flew off.
Those that had so valiantly sacrificed themselves floated
away. Lorna was left to try to soothe her poor throbbing
body.

The badger came up, squealing a greeting. His black

and white coat was also studded liberally with bees, but his body didn't even smart. He regarded Lorna in the water. 'Are you trying to swim?'

The lioness was so racked by pain that every other sense was obliterated. She didn't hear the badger, she couldn't see him and even a trace of his special scent failed to penetrate her swollen nose. At length the pain finally began to subside. Lorna got to her feet and shook herself.

'You look different,' the badger remarked. 'Sort of puffy. And your eyes are nearly closed.'

'I'm on fire,' the lioness groaned. 'I feel as if I've been eaten alive.'

'You have to be careful of bees if you have no defence against them. They don't bother me.'

'So I've you to thank for the torment I've just suffered, have I?' Lorna looked angry but she was too exhausted by her recent experience to do anything except complain. Ratel knew it and didn't budge.

'I'm sorry to see you so out of sorts,' he said. 'And you haven't even had the pleasure of the honey to make up for it.'

'Honey?' Lorna grunted. 'What's that? A kind of meat?'

'No.'

'Whatever it is, it isn't worth what I've endured to get at it. If you'd come hunting with me, none of this would have happened.'

'Sorry, but I can't resist the stuff. I *am* a honey badger.'

'Really? Well, I'm a *meat* lion. And that's all.' Lorna pulled herself out of the stream and, still grumbling mightily, plodded to her cave.

'Shall I – um – rustle something up for you?' the badger offered.

'No. I couldn't eat anything. How could I feel hungry after all that? You can just rustle off!'

The badger was enjoying seeing the vulnerable side of Lorna for once. She always appeared to be so in command on other occasions. He didn't feel real sympathy because he was incapable of appreciating how painful bee-stings could be. But he marvelled at the way some tiny insects had brought the massive beast so low. Even humans had so far failed to do that.

. . . And Hunted

Lorna nursed her sores and her hurt pride for a while. She didn't feel like hunting. The sheep farmer began to think that the threat to his animals was lifted. But eventually Lorna's appetite returned with a vengeance. She set off at once for the pasture, her mouth watering at the prospect of devouring another fat sheep. The honey badger had steered clear of the cave while Lorna was moping. He guessed she wanted to be left alone. Lorna didn't look out for him as she travelled through the forest. She wasn't looking for companionship. So it was quite by chance that they encountered each other that night. Their paths crossed near the edge of the woodland.

'Lion, don't go that way!' the badger cried at once. 'It's not safe!'

Lorna glared. 'What are you talking about, Ratel?'

'There are fierce animals guarding the fluffy ones,' the badger warned. 'They yelled at me and their yells brought some humans running. I saw sense and gave up the hunt. I'd rather stay free and eat mice.'

'Fierce animals?' Lorna mocked. 'What kind of fierce animals live round here apart from me?'

'Well, maybe they wouldn't bother *you*,' the honey badger allowed. 'But what of the humans? I've never trusted them. I think it's a trap.'

Lorna sat on her haunches and considered. 'Perhaps you're right about that,' she said. 'I must keep one step ahead.' She growled, angered by having her favourite prey placed out of bounds.

'You look as though you're back to your old self,' the honey badger remarked. 'Your face is—'

Lorna snarled. 'Don't remind me of all that!' She remembered the pain. She stood up. 'The humans have made a mistake if they think they can restrict me,' she declared. 'There will be other prey not so well guarded, I think.'

'You mean . . . *outside* the forest?' the badger asked.

'What do you think I mean? There's nothing to challenge me in here, is there?'

Ratel gasped. 'You'd actually go searching for this prey under the noses of the humans?'

Lorna purred, pleased with the badger's reaction. 'It won't be under their noses,' she replied, 'if they don't know I'm coming.' She turned and padded away unhurriedly towards a different section of the forest. The badger watched her for a while, then trotted after her.

The lioness made a wide detour around the sheep pasture and emerged from the woodland at a point where there was more open country. Here was hilly terrain interspersed with some pockets of farmland. Lorna had travelled purposefully, never looking back, but she suspected her badger friend was too inquisitive to let her go alone. A strong wind was blowing from the west. It was a warm wind and it carried with it a strong mix of scents, amongst which Lorna detected the rich odour of comfortable, well-fed beasts. She paused to listen for their voices, needing some guidance before she went further. The wind drowned most sounds. There was, however, one faint but insistent animal cry. Lorna didn't recognise it except in so far

as it sounded like a beast in pain. It was the clue she
wanted. Without turning her head she said, 'If you're
there, Ratel, this is the way to go,' and set off down a
slope towards the source of the cry.

The honey badger was amused. 'She knows me all
right,' he muttered to himself.

At the bottom of the slope they found a hedge; an
impenetrable tangle of thick thorn. Lorna patrolled its
length, looking for a possible opening, but found none.
She snarled with vexation. It seemed to the hungry
lioness that there was food to be had on the other side
if only she could get to it. She tried to assess the height
of the hedge in the darkness. She could see that it was
too high to leap over.

The animal cries had stopped. They had come from
a cow in labour; the calf was delivered now and mother
and baby were occupied with each other. The smell of
the new-born calf, though it was some distance away in
a barn, was very strong, for the straw on which the calf
had dropped was heavily impregnated with its scent.
The lioness knew she had to climb the hedge to reach
it, but thorns and prickles deterred her. She growled
louder and louder, exasperated with the obstacle.

'There's no avoiding discomfort here,' the honey
badger stated. 'Go on, lion. You'll be up and over
before you know you're hurt.'

'Easy for you to say,' Lorna snapped irritably, 'with
your weird thick skin.'

'All right,' said Ratel. 'I'll show you how.' He grasped
a stout branch and began to claw his way up. He was
an excellent climber and in no time he had reached
the top. 'Nothing to it,' he announced, 'but keep your
eyes closed.' He climbed just as easily down the other
side.

Lorna still hesitated. The thorns reminded her of
the bee-stings, ready to pierce and prick her. She had

suffered severely last time and was loath to risk further injury. She growled furiously at the badger, the hedge and herself. 'I'll have to find another way,' she roared finally and set off to seek some way of circumventing the thorns.

The badger fairly glowed, revelling in his superiority. 'I'm ahead of the lion,' he whispered to himself. 'The first choice must be mine.'

Dawn glimmered in the east as the determined little animal followed the calf's scent. He heard Lorna's roars of frustration rumbling beyond the man-made barrier. Some cattle stood in a field, cropping grass where it grew thickest. Despite their size, Ratel was not afraid of them. Only humans had the power to frighten him. He reached the barn where the black and white cow was suckling her new calf and trotted in, disturbing the peaceful atmosphere. The cow swung round to face him, putting herself between the interloper and her offspring. She lowed a warning, dropping her massive head.

The badger was undeterred. He ran around, aiming nips at the beast's legs and completely unsettling the calf, who bleated in its fright. The slow, heavy mother turned this way and that, trampling the straw and bellowing alarm. Outside, the other cattle raised their heads and tensed, sensing the danger. It was growing lighter by the minute. The badger had left it too late; the cow's mooing had been heard by the herdsman, who was already on his way and now increased his pace. The man's boots rattled on the path and he called in a deep rasping voice, 'I'm coming. Don't fret, Delia. I'm coming!'

The badger froze, then took to his heels as the man clattered into the barn, brandishing a long-handled broom at the intruder. It wasn't sufficiently light yet for the honey badger to be identified as the alien that he

was in the English countryside. The herdsman merely
saw a black and white animal scooting past him and
mistook him for his native European relative who was
no stranger in that part of the world.

'Come to pinch her milk, have you?' the man
shouted, voicing a belief that still persists in some areas.
Ratel felt a thump on his rear and he darted away with
a squeal.

'Ah! You didn't like that! Well, don't come back!'
The herdsman turned to settle the cow and her calf
down after their scare, and the honey badger ran back
to the thorn hedge where he lost no time in climbing
back to the other side. Lorna was nowhere in sight.

'Lion! Lion! I'm going back to the forest. Where are
you?'

Lorna didn't answer. She was far away. She had
reached the limit of the thorn hedge in one direction
where it turned at a right-angle to lead up to the farmhouse. She paced alongside it, obstinately refusing to
give up until she had found a gap.

The farmer's wife was drawing back the bedroom
curtains just as Lorna arrived. The lioness had found
her gap. The hedge gave way to a gate and Lorna's
tawny head could be seen peering through the bars as
the woman looked out of the window. There was a
shriek and a stammered cry. The woman pointed with
a trembling finger. 'L-look. Look there!'

The farmer rushed to the window, then hurtled
downstairs with a curse. 'Mind the children!' he yelled
behind him. He reached for his gun.

Lorna saw the woman gesticulating at the window.
She knew she was at risk, but at the same time she was
almost mesmerised by the ripe animal smells from the
new birth in the barn. She couldn't ignore them and
they drew her forward. The next instant the farmer
burst from the house, waving his arms and shouting at

the top of his voice. His gun, naturally, had been left unloaded, and he needed a few moments to arm it. Lorna backed away from the gate, snarling angrily. The man fumbled with his gun; his hands were shaking. Lorna saw her path to her intended prey was barred. For a brief moment she considered confronting the human, but instinct told her to avoid him. She turned and loped away, back along the obstructing hedge.

'Now's my chance,' the farmer murmured as he snapped his shotgun shut. 'This'll make her smart a bit!' He fired quickly at the retreating lioness. Lorna heard the crack of the gun and accelerated. Something whined past her ear. There was a second crack and the pellet skimmed through her back fur, slightly searing her skin. She growled and raced for the tree-line. The farmer didn't bother to reload. He stamped back to the farmhouse and telephoned the police.

Lorna was wild with disappointment and Ratel knew it. For the first time he felt vulnerable in the lioness's company. She had caught nothing and her eyes gleamed hungrily. In the daylight deer were difficult to stalk and the badger realised he offered an easy substitute.

'I'll leave you,' he said bluntly. 'We should get to our dens.'

Lorna didn't answer and the smaller animal's nerves tingled in alarm. He imagined Lorna was preparing to pounce. The badger scuttled into the brushwood to hide, wishing he hadn't lingered under the trees when he heard the gunshots. He peeped through the clustering vegetation to see if he was being hunted. Lorna was standing and looking towards him; a small red patch showed on her back hair. She was panting, and her eyes seemed to bore into him. He shrank down, waiting for the charge.

'Come out, Ratel. Don't be foolish. You don't need to hide from me,' Lorna boomed.

'How do *I* know that?' he asked nervously.

'Because I wouldn't waste my time trying to chew your tough hide,' Lorna replied in a bored tone. 'I've a much better plan in my head.'

'What's that?'

'Come out and I'll tell you,' the lioness continued slyly. 'I can't see you properly.'

'That's what I hoped,' said the honey badger. 'I – er – think I'll just stay in here a while, lion. At least, for as long as you're hungry.'

'Then you'll have a long wait. I shan't return to the hunt until nightfall, when those interfering humans will be sound asleep.'

All day long in the cave Lorna thought she could smell calf. The scent was in her nostrils, maddening her. She paced up and down her lair, unable to rest for a minute. Water drooled from her mouth and she grumbled to herself, growling constantly. The honey badger hadn't quite kept to his word. He had moved from his temporary shelter to his favourite burrow and there he had lain low. Dusk came slowly. Lorna stood at the threshold of the cave and roared at the darkening sky. She remembered her sister, but she had almost forgotten the zoo.

'Sister! Sister! Why are we no longer together?'

In the cave a faint echo of her cries could be heard as though there was an answering roar from the refuge at Kamenza: 'Why have they parted us?'

——9——

Injury

Ellen had eaten almost nothing for a week. She drank milk or water and spent most of her time resting in the shade and pining for her sister. Joel had been unable to tempt her to eat any substantial rations. The lioness was growing weaker and weaker. Joel knew that only Lorna could save her sister and he wanted to devote himself to reuniting them. He prepared to leave Kamenza.

Simon Obagwe brought him an up-to-date report on Lorna. 'She was seen at a dairy farm only yards from the farmhouse,' he told Joel. 'The farmer thinks she was after a young calf.'

Joel gasped. 'What happened?'

'He managed to drive her off, but he thinks she'll be back. He's asked for police assistance.'

'Oh no!' Joel groaned. 'They'll shoot her.'

Simon looked grim. 'Possibly, if she's a danger to the family as well.'

'I wish I'd gone sooner!' Joel exclaimed anxiously. 'I might have saved her. Now they'll both die.'

'Hold on, hold on.' Simon held up a hand. 'Nothing's happened yet. You'll be back in England within twenty-four hours. Perhaps you can still do some good? Why don't you contact the press people and get them to persuade the police to stay their hand until you're on the scene? They could keep Lorna at bay by putting down raw meat.'

'They've tried that,' Joel replied. 'It didn't work. She left it. Unless' – a thought struck him – 'unless it could be a dead animal, completely untouched. I believe Lorna associates raw meat too much with the fact that humans supply it. She just might accept a dead farm animal.'

'Good thinking,' Simon concurred. 'I reckon you should telephone right now.'

They turned to watch Simon's nine-year-old daughter Annie running across the yard to Ellen's pen. The girl was full of sympathy for the unhappy lioness and could often be found talking to her through the enclosure fence. Annie sat down and began to speak.

'I wish you didn't look so sad and I wish I could help you. I'd like to make you happy.'

At first Ellen hardly noticed the girl who chattered on as usual in the hope of comforting her, but eventually the lioness gave Annie her attention. The girl was always thrilled when she received that solemn, steady gaze. She gazed back, trying hard to make her own expression convey her sympathy.

'I wonder if you understand my feelings for you?' Annie whispered.

That night Ellen lay with her head on her paws, close to the entrance to her enclosure. She felt listless and abandoned. Even Joel had left her now. The African night with all its strange sounds hardly penetrated her consciousness. Upesi the cheetah patrolled her own pen. Every time she passed Ellen she cast a curious glance at her. She couldn't comprehend the strange animal that had been placed next to her, with all her troubles and sorrow.

'Why are you moping there?' the cheetah asked at

last, stopping to stare. 'The night's the time for movement. Don't you ever feel lively?'

Ellen looked up miserably. 'Never,' she moaned. 'Not
here.'

'Are you ill?'

'I think I am. I *feel* I am.'

'Why don't you eat your meat? Do they give you too
much?'

'What?' Ellen was barely listening. 'Oh. No, they
don't give me too much. I'm simply not hungry.'

'Well, why are you given it? They could give it to me.
I could eat more.'

'You're welcome to it,' said Ellen. 'There's only one
thing I want. I want my sister back. Nothing else is of
any use. I want her here with me. That's all. The way
it used to be.'

'Your sister, your sister! You never talk of anything
but your sister,' Upesi complained irritably. 'Why is she
so important to you?'

Ellen sighed. She thought for a while. The cheetah
turned away to continue her patrolling. 'Because,' said
Ellen, halting Upesi as she turned, 'without my sister I
don't feel whole.'

'I never know what you're talking about,' the cheetah
grunted. She had no siblings.

Joel left Kamenza and the African continent, not
knowing if he would be successful in his bid to stop
Lorna being destroyed. The newspaper campaign to
save the lionesses had turned sour in the light of recent
events. No one from the paper could promise that
any plea from that quarter would influence the police
involvement. They agreed to try; no more than that.
Public safety was paramount and they had to abide by
any decision taken by the police force. Joel had stressed
that both lionesses would die if they couldn't be

brought together again. Ellen had not adapted to her African quarters; Lorna was her only hope. There was no chance of releasing Ellen into the wild on her own. She wouldn't survive more than a day or so. She had never hunted prey and was now too weak and uninterested to accept any attempt by humans to give her hunting lessons. Lorna alone could do that.

On the long flight back to England Joel thought about the coming night. He knew it was critical. It would be another twelve to eighteen hours before he could get himself to Lingmere, by which time he might be too late to save Lorna. He tried to read but found himself staring at a blur of words on the page which his brain refused to absorb. He gave up and looked out of the window, willing the aircraft to gobble up the miles.

Night fell. Lorna's patience was exhausted. She set off with tremendous eagerness, fully confident that this time there would be no bar to her taking the succulent calf. The honey badger was watching out for her. He wanted to be in at the kill. He saw her huge lithe body looming in the twilight as she hastened along the much-used path. The badger swung in behind her, running quickly to keep up. Lorna was in a hurry. Ratel guessed the lioness was intent on rectifying her earlier mistake. He knew she felt cheated and wouldn't be comfortable until she had satisfied her pride. He hoped to have a portion of the tender meat she had set her sights on himself.

At the thorn hedge the badger started to climb again. Lorna, who hadn't acknowledged his presence until then, growled threateningly. 'No! Not that way, my friend. You must come the long way round like me!'

The badger, halfway up the hedge, stopped and considered. So the lioness was afraid he would reach the prey first? Perhaps he would. Would it be worth his while to take this chance of purloining the choicest parts? He weighed the pros and cons. Lorna's snarls grew in fierceness as he hesitated. The badger enjoyed the idea of scoring over the lioness, but he feared the consequences. Slowly he clambered down.

'Very wise,' Lorna commented. 'I doubt if you would have seen daylight again if you had crossed me.'

'Probably not,' the badger answered, unperturbed. 'Lead on, lion.'

'Complete silence now,' Lorna urged as she once again caught the scent of prey. She stalked alongside the hedge, slightly irritated by the rustling of the badger's feet behind her. Her eyes picked out an animal lying as still as death against the lowest thorns. She dropped to her belly and crawled forward cautiously. The animal didn't move. It was quite dead. When the lioness realised this she hurried forward again.

A still-born lamb had been placed deliberately to forestall Lorna's designs on the calf. The police had obtained the dairy farmer's agreement to the plan following the newspaper's request. The natural casualty had been procured from the nearby sheep flock and it was hoped this would serve to distract the lioness until her old keeper arrived the next day. However, in case the ruse didn't work, two police officers stood on guard on the farm ready to shoot if they had to.

Lorna sniffed at the body hungrily. It was a small meal for her, but she was ravenous and couldn't ignore it. She snatched up the carcass and ran back to the cover of the trees. The honey badger trotted after her hopefully.

Lorna snarled at him. 'There will be none for you, Ratel.' She busied herself with tearing off the remnants of wool while the badger watched. 'No more than a morsel for a lion. Find your own prey.'

Ratel had had an idea. 'All right, I will,' he said. He turned his back on Lorna and trotted down the slope once more towards the thorn hedge. He heard the crunch of bones as the lioness's powerful jaws dismembered the tiny lamb. Lorna was too absorbed with her meal to notice where the badger was heading. 'First to the prize after all,' he murmured to himself.

He scaled the prickly hedge easily, just as before, and made for the barn. Nobody on guard was on the lookout for a small animal like a badger. He slipped through the darkness, arousing no more than a passing interest from a fox on the prowl for rabbits. Every so often Ratel stopped in his tracks. It wouldn't be long before Lorna would have devoured the lamb and be on his tail. He listened carefully. He was excited.

The barn was closed. There was no way in now for a lion, but it was an old barn, and some of the boards were damaged. There were gaps for a small animal to wriggle through; the honey badger was capable of squeezing through surprisingly small spaces. He found one that would serve and scrambled through. The cow and her calf lay in a corner, the cow peacefully chewing some hay. The badger listened carefully. All he could hear was the champing of her teeth.

'She doesn't suspect yet,' the badger chortled to himself. 'What a din there will be when the lion discovers I've played a trick on her!'

Mother and calf got to their feet, suddenly sensing danger. The badger trotted forward and at once the cow began to stamp nervously and moo. The calf echoed her alarm. The badger was about to dart between them when there was a tremendous roar in the distance which he recognised at once. He stood rooted to the spot. Lorna was calling him. She was furious.

The men keeping watch on the farm tightened their grips on their weapons. Powerful lights were switched on. Their beams swept the farmyard and the farm's precincts, pasture and meadow, while Lorna continued to roar. Ratel marvelled at the noise, his skin bristling. The cow and calf were terrified. The lioness, angry and vengeful, was climbing the thorn hedge, her anger overriding her discomfort. Her face was scratched, her skin torn, but she ignored the irritation. The cunning of the honey badger had surprised and riled her beyond bearing. She was not so much furious with him as furious with herself for failing to anticipate his deception. She teetered on the top of the hedge. Thorny twigs and stems snapped beneath her weight and showered to the ground as she steadied herself for a jump. Just then the beam of an arc lamp swung towards her and stopped, bathing her in light and dazzling her. Lorna roared again, this time with fright. Desperate to escape the blinding light, she struggled to free herself from its glare. There was no refuge on the farm side of the hedge, where most of the area was starkly illuminated; Lorna half jumped and half fell backwards into the comparative darkness behind her. Pierced and ripped by thorns, she howled with pain. Then she retreated to the woods to lick her wounds, limping noticeably from a large thorn caught in one of her paws.

There was no direct path that could be taken to follow her. By the time the armed men were on her trail, Lorna was well hidden. The deep darkness of the forest made pursuit difficult and dangerous, and the men reluctantly decided to abandon the search. With fear of capture removed, Lorna became more conscious of pain. She lay in some undergrowth and tried to bite the thorn free from her left hind foot. It was a very awkward manoeuvre; the thorn was too fine for her great teeth to grasp. She licked the place to soothe it, then continued on towards her lair.

By the time Lorna reached the cave, her paw was throbbing agonisingly. With each step the thorn had been driven further between her toes. She hobbled into her lair and lurched on to her side, keeping her injured foot free. Lorna gasped wearily and wondered how she could ever stalk prey again.

— 10 —

A Friendly Act?

The honey badger had been scared by the brilliant lights. He hadn't known where to run. He tried to skulk in a corner of the barn but the cow's continual mooing made him jittery. He thought that eventually some of the men would come to investigate, so when he heard them set off in pursuit of Lorna he made haste to get clear.

He got out of the barn and scurried back to the hedge. He wasn't sure where Lorna was and he knew she was angry with him. He needed to avoid her, at least until she had calmed down.

'That wasn't a clever trick,' he told himself. 'I gained nothing by trying to cheat her. Now she'll be hunting for *me*.' He climbed the hedge and carefully descended on the other side. 'She's so silent when she's hunting,' he muttered. 'She could be lying in wait anywhere.'

He couldn't catch her scent so, with distinct nervousness, he edged along the hedge bottom, constantly wondering if he would suddenly be crushed by the lioness leaping out at him from the darkness. Gradually, as the moments passed, the badger gained a little confidence. Maybe Lorna had forgiven him. If she had been hunting him, she surely would have found him by now. He felt easier and yet he was puzzled. Where could she have gone?

He returned to the forest and set about finding something to eat. Insects and a skinny frog were all that came his way that night. His concentration was upset and he spent as much time trying to locate Lorna as he did his prey. The forest, of course, was large and the lioness could have been anywhere. Yet the badger began to worry that somehow the humans had taken her.

'Only one way to find out,' he told himself. 'I must go to her lair.'

Some distance from it he knew Lorna was inside. He sensed her presence even before he heard her panting breaths. She was in distress, he could tell, and he approached more boldly than he otherwise would have done.

She heard him and was surprised to find herself relieved. 'Ratel! I wondered if you'd come.'

The honey badger paused at the entrance. 'Are you ill?' he asked. 'What has happened?'

'I got injured,' the lioness answered in an unusually plaintive voice. 'The thorns ripped at me. I've got one stuck in my foot. I can't get it out and it's lamed me.'

'Thorns?' the badger echoed. 'From the hedge?'

'Yes. I came after you. You must have heard me. I wanted to teach you a lesson, you treacherous little . . .' Lorna's voice subsided into a sigh but the badger began to back away none the less.

'I caught nothing,' he said. 'There were humans all around. But are you sure you're lame? How could you have got back here so easily?'

'I *didn't* get back here easily,' Lorna snarled. 'Every step was agony. Ratel, how can I hunt? I can't walk.'

'Let me see your injury. Perhaps I can help. Where is the thorn?' He inched forward, unsure if he would be permitted to enter the cave.

Lorna was past caring about that. 'You'll see nothing

in here,' she told him. 'It's far too dark. But you may
come in. I – I'd welcome your company.'

The honey badger had never before been treated
like this, not even in Lingmere. He trotted inside. 'Well
now, lion, this is a problem indeed,' he commented.
'When there is more light, I'll inspect your paw. I can
see which one is paining you, by the way you're lying.'
He glanced around at the scraps of bone and hide
littering the cave floor. 'You won't be doing any
pouncing for a while, will you? You can't make a leap
on three legs.'

'I know all that,' the lioness growled. 'I shall be
confined to catching prey that walks past my nose.'

'Whoops! Maybe I won't come so close,' the badger
remarked jocularly, but he didn't advance any further.

'I shall starve,' Lorna moaned. 'I can't live off beetles
and grubs.'

'I will bring you prey,' the badger said. 'There are
plenty of rabbits and birds and squirrels. I won't let
you starve, lion. We have always been friends, haven't
we?'

'Yes we have,' Lorna purred. 'Thank you, Ratel.'

'And when you've recovered,' the badger went on,
'we'll plot how we can trap that succulent, tender
animal we both want so much.'

Lorna snarled. 'The humans are guarding it. They
threw lightning at me and forced me away. They would
do the same again.'

The badger grinned, showing his powerful teeth. 'It
was night-time. What if we go by day?'

'You are cunning. But would it be sensible? Humans
are more active in the daylight.'

'Yes – too busy to wonder if we're coming.'

'We've tried both daylight and darkness,' Lorna
reminded him. 'Humans are always on guard, it seems.

I can't think about it now, Ratel. Pain wipes out everything else.'

'Do you want to sleep? If so, I'll go.'

'I *can't* sleep. My foot pounds so.'

'Unfortunate lion,' said the badger. 'I'm sorry for
you. Do you ever wish you were back in the care of
humans?'

'Until now, no. Now I don't know how I feel. But I
would like to see my sister again.'

On his way back to Lingmere Joel thought a lot about
the lionesses and how time was not on their side. When
he arrived he was relieved and gladdened by the news
that the police had stopped short of shooting Lorna.
Now he had a few days' grace in which to try to trace
her and coax her into the open. He believed she might
still respond to him in a way she would never do to
anyone else. That she would remember him he had no
doubt. Theirs was a long association and if anybody
could save the day, Joel knew it was himself. But the
news from Kamenza was not good. Ellen's fast continued and she was thin and weak.

Joel lost no time in acquainting himself with all the
places in the forest where Lorna had been sighted.
Martin accompanied him to the woodland and
described everything that had occurred there and how
his team had failed at every point. 'We needed you
here from the word go,' he finished.

'That might have been wiser, yes,' Joel agreed. 'There
was no time, though, to think about it. Things went
wrong from the outset.'

The team gathered together again with Joel as their
leader. They combed the woods, Joel calling the lioness
by name at regular intervals. He was confident of some
response from Lorna if he could only get to a spot
where she could hear him. Each time Joel called, the

men stood silently and strained their ears for a sound. When they heard nothing, they moved to another place.

'Lorna! Lorna! Lorna!'

The lioness heard the calls faintly from a distance, but the men were not sufficiently close for her to recognise Joel's voice. She stayed in the cave, only moving to hobble to the stream to drink. While there were humans around she kept herself hidden. The wound in her foot made her extremely vulnerable. If she were discovered in the open, she would not be able to run away.

The honey badger also heard the human cries. He emerged from his burrow at dusk and hunted for small mammals that were easy to carry to Lorna's lair. Mice, voles, squirrels and frogs were not a problem. Rabbits were too heavy so he ate those himself. Lorna's hunger was always with her. And her wound was festering.

'Is it any better?' the badger would always ask as he arrived with food.

'No. Worse,' was the invariable reply.

'Shall I try to bite the thorn?' Ratel asked eventually.

'You said before that you couldn't,' Lorna moaned. 'Besides, I'm much too sore to bear your teeth nibbling at me. If you had only done it at first . . .'

'You told me I couldn't see properly in your den,' the badger reminded her. 'Why didn't you come outside where I might have had a chance?'

'It wouldn't have made any difference if it was dark.'

'But in the daylight?'

'Men are about. You must have heard them. How could I risk it?'

'Well then, what will you do?'

Lorna's head dropped on to her front paws. 'I don't know,' she groaned. 'I can't think straight.'

'Well, I've brought prey. As much as I could manage,' the badger pointed out. 'Shall I fetch more?'

'Just as you like,' the lioness answered without interest.

'Come on, lion. Don't give up!' Ratel chided her. 'Think about that new-born animal . . .'

'I can't think about it!' Lorna snapped. 'I shan't ever get there!'

The honey badger gaped. The full implication of Lorna's wound sank in and he stared at her for a while without moving.

'What are you gawping at?' she growled irritably.

'I – um – nothing, really,' the badger mumbled. His thoughts were racing. 'I'll go and get more meat.' He hurried away, glad to be alone to think. A plan to help Lorna was forming in his head. 'It might be the only way out for her,' he said to himself. He paused to ponder a little. 'I'll be putting myself in danger,' he muttered, 'but if I do it right, it should work out.'

The next morning the badger squatted inside his burrow and listened to the human's calls. It was Joel's second day of searching and he and the team were threading through a different section of the forest. The badger heard them and Lorna heard them. Joel's voice was closer now and the lioness raised her head and tried to recall what was familiar about the sound. But she couldn't quite grasp it. Pain and misery took control again and she rolled back on to her side.

The honey badger's heart thumped quickly as he deliberately pulled himself from his den and looked carefully around.

'Lorna! Lorna!'

The badger heard but couldn't yet see the men. Then footsteps, crackles of twig and leaf and eventually the smell of men was detectable too. The badger waited, steeling himself to be still until he should catch a first glimpse of the party.

'I must be mad,' he murmured. 'I must be mad. I'll be sorry for this later, I know I will.' He gulped as he saw Joel, at the head of the group, stumping along a path through the trees. 'Now for it!' Ratel hissed and ran forward.

'Lorna! Lorna! Lor— Great heavens! Look, Martin!' Joel pointed in amazement as the honey badger ran across their path about twenty metres away.

'A honey badger!' croaked Martin. 'What on earth . . .'

'He's been here all along!' Joel cried in excitement. 'Let's follow him.'

'You'll never catch him.'

'He's stopped!' Joel yelled as he sprinted off. 'Come on, he's turned to look.'

The badger had indeed paused on purpose. He wasn't running away. Not yet. He had something else to do first. He watched the men lumbering after him, then set off again.

'Do you want to take him?' Martin panted. 'He'll never let us near . . . enough . . . to throw a net. Should . . . we leave him?'

'No. Why do that? He's probably heading for his den. If so, we'll have him cornered. We could dig him out.'

But the badger wasn't heading for his den, of course. He was heading for quite another place. Every so often he would stop just long enough to make sure the men weren't too far behind, then trot on. His tireless loping run had his pursuers badly out of breath in only a short time, but Joel wouldn't give up. It had occurred to him that since the badger and the lions had been close neighbours in the zoo it was possible that Lorna and the badger were living near each other in the forest.

Ratel neared the cave. His plan was for the men to find the lioness and take her into their care. He knew enough about humans to know that they could heal her. But he wanted Lorna to believe the men had found her by chance; he didn't want her to feel betrayed by her only friend. Somehow, he must lead the men to the cave and to Lorna before making his own escape.

The men were a long way behind when the honey badger reached the stream. Ratel waited as long as he dared, then growled loudly so that Lorna could hear him.

'Take care, lion. Humans are in the woods and may be coming this way.'

There was no answer from the cave.

'Can you hear me?' the badger whistled.

'Of course I can hear you,' Lorna roared.

At first, the badger thought he had done enough. The lion's roar had been unmistakable and Ratel could see the leader beckoning the rest of the team forward in a fever of impatience. But the man hadn't seen the cave; its entrance was camouflaged too well by the clinging plant growth. He was cautiously advancing on some thick undergrowth, believing that to be where Lorna was hidden. The badger watched in dismay. Did these blind humans need to be led literally into the lion's den? Terrified of being cornered himself, longing to flee, he came to an agonising decision. 'The men are after me,' he squealed, and ran right into the cave mouth.

'Don't bring them here!' roared Lorna, struggling to get to her feet. She yelped with pain as she put pressure on her injured foot, and fell back on the cave floor.

'She's in there!' Joel cried to the other men as he finally located the lair. 'We mustn't alarm her. I'll go first. Give me the air rifle.' He strode to the cave entrance. The honey badger was nowhere to be seen, having run as far back into the cave as he could and was crouching there in total darkness. But Joel could see the lioness, lying on her side by the stream. She snarled but made no effort to rise.

'There's something wrong here,' Joel whispered to Martin. 'I think she may be sick. Get the stretcher ready. I'm going in.' He crept forward, stooping as he entered. Even in the dim interior the lioness was an easy target. Joel knelt, fitted the dart and raised the rifle. Lorna remembered Ellen and reacted violently. Swinging round, she got on to her good feet, holding the bad one off the floor. Joel could see she was going to attack. Her muscles rippled.

'Lorna! Don't you know me?'

The lioness hesitated as she recognised her old keeper. Joel had just long enough to fire the dart and back away. It was all over in seconds. Lorna crashed to the floor as Joel got himself out of her range. For a while the lioness thrashed about, and then the drug took effect.

'Hurry!' Joel called. 'We must tie her and get her into the sling. She's quite quiet now. Leave the net for the badger.'

Lorna was rolled on to the stretcher. As they tied her limbs together they noticed the wound.

'Looks septic,' said Joel. 'We must attend to that.'

They hauled the lioness outside. Then Lorna was hoisted into the air, six men bearing her weight, three on either side, taking the poles of the sling on their shoulders. They gasped at the weight of her. Joel was left free. He took out his mobile phone. The carrier firm that had transported Ellen had been on standby for days; their vehicle was parked at the old zoo premises. 'We'll need a trailer,' Joel told Martin. 'I'll get them to bring one through the sheep pasture. You know – where Lorna first got away. It's a long haul, but we've got a couple of hours to get her to the zoo laboratory. I'll have the vet waiting. Can you do it?'

'Case of having to,' Martin grunted as the men staggered away with their burden.

Joel was already calling the carriers' mobile phone number. 'I'll try to take the badger,' he called after the stretcher crew. 'Africa's the place for him!'

Back to the Zoo

One quick call to the carriers' men and one to the vet got the immediate tasks organised. Joel turned his attention to the badger. He re-entered the cave, ducking down to a squat as he waited for his eyes to accustom themselves to the deeper blackness farther inside. He had no torch. His only hope was to attempt to drive the badger towards the entrance and catch him in the mesh of the net. The air in the cave was foul. Joel wrinkled his nose and noticed the debris of Lorna's prey littering the cave floor. He listened for sounds of the badger's movements, but there was silence. Joel knew he had little chance of success if he couldn't ascertain exactly where the badger was skulking. Even then the odds were stacked in the animal's favour. He couldn't be darted as Lorna had been. The dose was much too powerful for so small an animal. So Joel was relying entirely on the net to disable a beast that was noted for its tenacity. Moreover the badger's claws and teeth were capable of inflicting serious wounds.

Joel picked up a piece of bone and threw it into the dark depths. It rattled along the dry floor and was followed by a scraping noise. He remembered he had matches in his pocket. He lit one and held it at arm's length as it sputtered. A small section of the cave was illuminated. Joel inched forward and lit another match. The cave, he soon found, narrowed sharply farther inside. The badger hadn't passed him, so he knew it must be at the back of the cave and was now boxed in.

Ratel kept still. He had reached the limit of the cave and was pressed against its wall where the stream began to run underground. The piece of bone had skipped towards him and he had shifted just a little. His claws had scratched the rocky floor. He knew he was in a trap. He had sacrificed himself to get Lorna to safety. He remembered how the animals in Lingmere Zoo had been dealt with; how they had disappeared. Now a human was coming to grab him. But the badger liked the forest and wanted to stay in it. He wasn't going to go quietly. The man came on. One after another, flames briefly lit the cave. The fumes from them made the badger sneeze. The next flame showed the man to be very close. Ratel bared his teeth.

Joel got the net ready. He had one trick up his sleeve. He knew he could dazzle the animal momentarily if he held one match almost in his eyes. He struck the match, saw the badger and lunged forward, almost singeing the black and white fur. Then he threw the net and wrapped it close just as the animal recovered from the shock of the flame and began to kick. The badger had strong legs. Joel exerted all his strength. He felt the badger's claws trying to rip but dodged away. A piece of rope whipped round the netting and drawn tight put paid to the badger's struggles. Now the animal used its scent gland. In the confined space its strength was magnified. Joel backed hastily away, leaving the trussed badger where he was.

Emerging into the open air Joel drew several lungsful of fresh air into his body. He sat down, feeling strangely woozy. It was a while before he ventured back into the cave, and even then the musky smell permeated every corner. Joel held his breath and crawled forward again, feeling his way. He grabbed his live parcel and twisted round, desperate for clean air. Lugging the badger behind him, he dived for the cave opening. It wasn't until he was once more in the daylight that Joel could see what a truly splendid piece of wrapping he had done.

The badger's eyes glared at him with a glitter of rage. Joel chuckled. 'You've been humiliated, haven't you? All for the best in the long run. If only you knew where you are going!' He caught him up and set off. 'Now let's go and join the others.'

The men carrying Lorna had made good progress. Once on a proper path they had got into a steady rhythm and were marching along keeping their eyes peeled for the trailer that was to bring their relief. Joel came up with them, proudly showing off his trophy.

'Mmm. Quite a successful day,' Martin said. He was perspiring profusely as were all the men.

'I'll take a turn,' Joel offered. 'Anyone ready to do a swap?'

'It'll disturb our rhythm,' Martin replied. 'We'll keep going.'

A little later the trailer was spotted and the men brightened visibly. They called to those trundling it along the uneven path to speed up a bit. Soon afterwards Lorna and Ratel were lying side by side on the trailer. The men rubbed their strained arms and shoulders and mopped their faces. From then on their pace accelerated.

The lioness and the badger left the forest together. They would never see it again. The trailer was hitched to the Land-Rover and the animals headed for the

ghost zoo that was Lingmere. Ratel saw no sign of life
in Lorna. He wondered why she had been killed while
he had been left alive. He was reminded that it was a
foolish beast that tried to understand a human's
motives.

Lingmere Zoo was unchanged in appearance, except
for the absence of all the animals. The enclosures
hadn't yet been dismantled. While Lorna was rushed
into the lab for treatment by the waiting vet, Ratel
found himself back in his old cage. His bindings were
carefully removed. He dashed at once to a hiding-place,
growling his resentment.

'What do they want with me? Why am I to be kept
here again?' he groaned over and over. He had got
used to his freedom and the horribly swift change back
to incarceration was more than he could bear. 'I'm
alone here now. All the others have gone. Why are
humans so cruel?'

Lorna's paw was soon dealt with. The thorn was
removed, the wound drained of poison, cleaned and
sterilised. She was bandaged and left in her old
enclosure to recover.

'There shouldn't be any more infection,' said the
vet. 'We'll need to keep an eye on her for a day or so,
but she should be ready to travel in forty-eight hours.'

Joel got ready to fly back to Kamenza. News of Ellen
was much the same. No one gave her much of a chance.
Joel tried to picture the two lionesses together again
in the refuge. How different they would look: one
strong and healthy and bold, the other a thin, listless
shadow of her twin. Was there time for Ellen to recover?
The newspaper was preparing for a heartrending story.
Whether Ellen survived or succumbed, either way the
paper would have the attention of the nation.

*

Lorna woke and glanced around groggily. For a while she couldn't get her bearings. So many strange and frightening things had happened in the last day. But eventually she realised where she was. She staggered to her feet, swaying unsteadily, and stared at her bandaged foot. The foot was tender but no longer sent a stab of sharp pain through her body. She remembered the cave and the hours she had spent lying on her side. Somehow the easing of pain and her return to her old quarters were connected. Lorna's head swung round slowly. She was familiarising herself again with the enclosure's features. There was something wrong with the place. Lorna blinked and tried hard to think what it was. In her muzzy state it was a while before she realised what was missing. Then she gave a little cry of distress. Ellen wasn't there. For the first time she was alone in her old home. Now there was no forest, no prey, no hunting prowess to distract her. Just as when she had first hidden herself in the forest, Lorna roared aloud her sense of isolation. She roared for Ellen who seemed lost to her for ever.

Her roars were answered not by other roars, but by the surprised and excited chirrups of the honey badger. 'Lion! Lion! It's me – Ratel. You're back again,' he chattered. 'I thought you were dead. Can you see me? I'm at the front of the cage as I used to be. Come and talk!'

Lorna limped across and pressed her head against the fence. Across the pathway the honey badger was trotting up and down excitedly in his own cage. Lorna recalled how the humans had come to her lair in the wake of the badger's arrival.

'You tricked me, Ratel,' she accused him. 'Why did you lead the men to me?' She sounded forlorn and hurt.

'To rescue you. You would never have left your lair again. Your freedom is gone – like mine – but you're alive. I'm so relieved. I thought at first that the men had killed you. I couldn't understand why only I was allowed to survive. Are you still in pain?'

'A little. Ratel, I wish you had left me to perish in my den.'

'How could I? We're friends, aren't we?'

'Yes, we're friends. But what sort of life will this be after our adventures in the forest?'

'Well – as it always was, I suppose. Safe. Boring. And tame.'

'It's not as it always was,' Lorna contradicted. 'It can never be that so long as my sister is missing.'

'No. I'd forgotten,' the badger said softly. He heard a rattle along the path. 'Oh-oh, look. We're going to be fed.' He disappeared from sight as the food trolley approached. Lorna was given extra rations to build her up. The badger received some odd cuts off the same carcass. The lioness limped to the food and was soon absorbed. There was very little that could deter her from eating.

How different the situation was with her sister! Ellen languished in her pen in Kamenza. She was at a very low ebb. People there thought she had simply given up and was waiting to die. Annie spent every spare moment with her and Ellen did seem to respond to her kindness. She would creep forward and put her head close to the fence to listen to Annie's voice. But that was all. The girl had no more success persuading Ellen to look at her food than anyone else. They had tried everything to make her eat. She was now so weak that even feeding by hand had been attempted; Ellen had refused all sustenance except milk. It was the only thing that was keeping her alive and, because she didn't reject it, Simon Obagwe was able to help her by adding vitamins and other dietary essentials to the liquid. But Ellen had almost no real strength. Her flesh hung loose, her coat was patchy and her eyes were dull and uninterested. She showed no curiosity and no change of mood, only listlessness.

When news of Lorna's recapture reached Kamenza, there was some optimism in the refuge. The staff made renewed efforts to persuade Ellen to eat; they were afraid that she might die before Lorna could be brought out. Annie urged the weakling to drink extra milk and Ellen did accept an additional pailful. Now everyone went around with crossed fingers, willing the lioness to stay alive for just a few more days. They all hoped the sight of her sister would work a transformation in her, but they also feared that, by the time of Lorna's arrival, Ellen would be too weak to ever make a proper recovery.

Upesi the cheetah had observed the lioness's decline day by day. It was a complete mystery to her. She was impatient and scornful of Ellen's illness. She watched the supplies of meat delivered to the lioness's pen and she watched the dried-up, fly-covered, untasted food taken out again. The absurdity of it really aggravated her. It was pointless and ridiculous.

'Give it to me,' she would snarl at the humans as they tried with such regularity to tempt the obstinate Ellen. 'Give it to me. *I'll* eat it. That's what you want, isn't it? For it to be eaten? Why waste it on her? You know she's going to refuse it. *Give it to me!*' But she knew they never would and it made her mad.

The men ignored her snarls. They thought she was bad-tempered. Even Ellen protested.

'Can't you be quieter?' the lioness complained feebly. 'Always growling at me. I only ask for some peace, nothing more.'

'All right,' said Upesi. 'I'll stop talking altogether. I can see you take no interest in anything. I waste my breath on you; that's quite clear. Huh! It's like talking to a tree.' She continued pacing around her enclosure until it was too hot to do more than seek out a shady spot and go to sleep.

Ellen was grateful for the times when Upesi slept and there was almost no noise of any kind except for the buzzing of insects or a lazy cry from one man to another as they made their rounds. Then Ellen would day-dream. She would imagine she and her sister were lying side by side under the trees, happy in each other's company, knowing they would be undisturbed. The peace and contentment of such a scene would soon lull her to sleep. And while Ellen slept, Lorna's paw was healing and the hour drawing near for Joel to escort her to Kamenza.

——12——

Airlift

Arrangements for transporting Lorna were completed. The truck to carry her to the airport stood ready. The honey badger was already crated after a long struggle to catch him inside his cage. Lorna had to be sedated and the men were not going to make the same mistake with her twice. Joel had suggested they should wait until she was asleep, to avoid complications. Approaching the lioness was doubly difficult now. Although she knew her old keeper and recognised her name, Lorna had reverted almost entirely to the wild creature she was. Luckily, the weather was hot and humid which made her drowsy. It was left to Joel to sedate her.

When she was quiet he crept inside the enclosure. Lorna lay on her side. Her sore paw had healed beautifully and scarcely troubled her. This time the darting was easy because Joel was able to get close. As soon as the needle had gone in, he leapt away for the gate because Lorna was on her feet the moment she felt the dart. She complained angrily as Joel dashed through the exit. A few minutes later she was comatose.

In the next quarter of an hour Lorna was crated and she and the badger were packed inside the truck alongside each other. They set off for the airport at once, Joel travelling in the cab of the vehicle.

'I hope the rest of the journey goes as smoothly,' he said to the driver. 'Time is the critical factor now.'

In Kamenza Simon Obagwe and his staff were counting the hours to evening when Joel and Lorna were due to arrive. It was a momentous day all round, for a little earlier Upesi the cheetah had been released on to the plains. For days now her supply of raw meat had been reduced – triggering her impatience with Ellen – and she had been killing small mammals brought to her pen for her to hunt, until the wardens judged her ready to make her way in the wild. Outside her pen, however, everything was strange, and Upesi had not yet emerged from the shelter of some long grass. Ellen hadn't noticed the cheetah's absence. These days Ellen was almost always asleep.

In the gloom of the lorry's interior, the badger moved nervously around his crate. He could smell the lioness close by and, just as before, wondered at her silence. But he knew this time that she wasn't dead. He understood now that the humans could make an animal quiet and still any time they chose. He waited anxiously for Lorna to recover. He didn't like being confined in this cramped way and he was frightened by the vehicle's noise and movement. What on earth were the humans planning to do with them this time? They had hardly got used to their old quarters again before they were roughly removed. Ratel thought he had been treated quite brutally. He had put up strong resistance and had evaded the men for as long as he could. But there had seemed to be an army of them this time and in the end they were too many for him. Struggle as he would, they overpowered him with real force and locked him away in this tiny container. He felt as though he could hardly breathe. He stared at the dark shape of the lioness slumped in a corner of her much larger crate. He thought he could hear her murmuring to herself, but she was only drawing deep breaths as she laboured back to consciousness.

'I wish you'd talk,' the honey badger muttered. 'I'm feeling panicky here on my own. Why are the humans bothering with me?'

The lorry droned on. The badger tried to sleep.

Lorna awoke on the aircraft. The transfer from truck to plane had gone smoothly. Joel was delighted and, as they sat on the tarmac awaiting clearance, Lorna's first drowsy growls could be heard.

'I'm here,' said Ratel. 'Still here and still your friend. But badly scared and really glad I've got you for company at last.'

'Ah. I'm glad too,' Lorna mumbled. 'I'm so tired. What's the matter with me? Why am I in this thing? Where's the—'

'We've been imprisoned by the humans,' the badger quickly broke in. 'Only they know why. We're at their mercy. But I don't think they mean us any harm. The usual man is with us.'

'The one who talks to us? *He's* no threat. But I shall escape again as soon as I can and go back to the forest.'

'I don't even know where that is any more,' the badger told her. 'We've been bumped around and whisked about so much that I've forgotten how to get there. We must be patient and wait for the right moment, lion. Freedom once won mustn't be lost again.' His final remark was drowned by the aircraft's engines bursting into life. They were on the move again.

The animals were fed and watered during the flight. Their cramped conditions made them miserable and fractious. As the sedative wore off Lorna began to blame the badger.

'This is your doing,' she snarled weakly. 'If it wasn't for you I wouldn't be stuck in this box, aching in every limb.'

The badger was hurt. 'Maybe you would and maybe you wouldn't,' he said. 'Maybe you'd have starved to death. The humans would have found you anyway eventually, dead or alive.'

'Better in my den than in this horrible place,' Lorna sighed.

The honey badger bristled. 'Let me remind you of something, lion. I didn't have to help you. I sacrificed my own freedom too when I entered your den. There was no way out again. The humans saw to that.'

'More fool you, then.'

'Yes. I was foolish,' said Ratel, 'to expect any gratitude from you.'

Lorna put her head on her paws. She remembered what the pain in her foot had been like. Now it hardly troubled her. It was difficult for her to apologise. She didn't want to be beholden to a far smaller creature than herself. 'I suppose, Ratel, we ought to stop squabbling,' she murmured. That was as far as she could go.

'Of course we should,' the honey badger agreed readily. 'We're in this together and we should take comfort from that.'

'All right,' said Lorna.

It was evening when the plane touched down in Africa. There was quite a crowd to greet the newcomers. Lorna's arrival was the cause of excitement locally; news had spread of the ailing lioness in Kamenza who was about to be saved by her long-lost sister. The honey badger was less of a celebrity.

Simon Obagwe had acted to ensure that Lorna's

introduction to Kamenza was a low-key affair. There were to be no photographers or crowds of any sort in the refuge when the lioness was put with her sister. They were to be given every chance to settle down peacefully before any publicity teams arrived from the British or the local press. But now, at the airport, Joel waved to the smiling, gesticulating onlookers as Lorna and Ratel were offloaded from the aircraft. He was in a state of considerable excitement himself and he felt as if he had reached the conclusion of a difficult period. Whatever happened now, the sisters would be together. He had done everything possible to bring that about. His job was almost over.

'All set?' he asked Paul, his driver, with a grin.

'Can't wait,' Paul answered happily, 'to see the look on Ellen's face.'

Joel nodded. 'Or Lorna's,' he murmured.

Simon and Joel swapped relieved stories as they wrung each other's hands at Kamenza. 'She's holding on,' were Simon's first words.

Everyone at the refuge wanted to see Lorna join her sister lioness. Annie was dancing with excitement. She clung to her mother's hand and hopped from one foot to the other. But first Ratel was put into Upesi's old pen. The badger instantly disappeared from sight.

'Digging,' Simon commented with a rueful smile.

'We owe that little creature quite a lot,' Joel said with a hint of affection. 'As I told you on the phone, he really found Lorna for us.'

And then the great moment arrived. Lorna, still crated, was placed inside the enclosure where Ellen lay on her side under a bush, breathing deeply. It was darkening, but Joel could see how emaciated she was. The onlookers held their breath as Lorna's crate was opened and the huge lioness, looking almost twice the size of her unfortunate sister, stepped from it uncertainly. It was obvious that she didn't yet see that another animal was already occupying the pen. She looked back at the men removing the crate, who were quickly fastening the lock of the enclosure gate behind them, and growled, unsure of what would happen next.

The people stood back, willing her on. They wanted to see the lionesses reunited before darkness made them invisible. Annie could hardly keep still. Lorna moved slowly, warily. Then, suddenly, she spotted the sleeping Ellen. She froze, growling low in her throat. Ellen awoke and looked up. The lionesses stared at one another. Neither moved a muscle. Lorna seemed to be trying to catch a scent. She was testing the air. She growled again and this time there was a low, feeble answering call from Ellen. Lorna moved forward more confidently, walking directly up to her sister. Ellen stood up, swaying slightly. Lorna reached her and nuzzled her, uttering a soft half growl, half purring sound.

'She knows her!' someone whispered tensely.

It was an emotional moment for everybody. The lionesses were talking to each other, nuzzling and licking each other's faces in a kind of ecstasy. Ellen soon had to lie down again, and Joel's eyes smarted as her sister at once crouched next to her and put a protective paw across her shoulders. He dared not trust his voice. It was over. He had done it! As the darkness deepened the onlookers walked away, leaving the sisters at peace.

Lorna knew her sister by her smell and her call. Ellen's appearance, of course, was very much altered. When the humans had gone – Annie lingering until her mother had to drag her away – Lorna raised the subject.

'Sister, what's wrong? Are you ill?'

'Not now,' Ellen purred. 'I've been waiting for you.'

'You're so weak. Have the men been cruel?'

'No. They've fed and cared for me as much as in our old home.'

'Then what—'

'I couldn't eat,' said Ellen. 'I can't live alone, sister. I thought you were lost. I don't know why I had to spend this time on my own. But I waited and waited . . .'

'And I thought you were dead,' Lorna murmured. 'I escaped from the old home and lived my life in the forest. I thought of you many, many times.'

Ellen couldn't grasp what she was hearing. 'You lived . . . in the forest? Where's that?' Lorna explained. 'But how did you survive?' Ellen persisted. 'You were *alone?*'

'Not quite,' Lorna answered. 'Ratel escaped too. We hunted together sometimes.'

'You have a tale to tell,' Ellen said. 'I long to hear it. But first, I am going to eat. There's meat in that corner. There has always been meat. I never could face it before. I felt as though half of me had been left behind with you, wherever you were. Now I'm – *we're* – whole again. With you here, sister, I've got my life back.'

—— 13 ——

Recovery

Even by the next morning Ellen seemed different. Of course she was as thin as ever but, for the first time since her arrival, she seemed interested in what was going on around her. She was more alert than anyone had seen her before. Lorna, on the other hand, was angry and embittered towards the humans. She had known freedom and now she was confined again. She snarled furiously whenever any of the staff stopped to look or passed nearby.

'This place is no better than the old one we used to think of as home,' she complained to Ellen. 'Why were we moved here? We must escape.'

Ellen, who had only known human care, wasn't alarmed. 'We can manage here, can't we?' she asked. 'I don't understand any other way. You told me life was harder in the forest. You were injured. And at least we're together.'

'No. We can't manage here, sister,' Lorna corrected her. 'I can't accept this dreary kind of existence where nothing is real. Where you saunter around the extent of your world and when you've done it you do it all over again because there is nothing else. Where you wait to be fed instead of finding prey when you want to. There's something in the air here that seems to be beckoning me, but it's beyond this ... this ... false world. Don't you feel it too?'

Ellen thought and she did remember a strange, indefinable feeling that had gripped her on her arrival: a feeling almost of familiarity, as though she were returning from afar. It was impossible to comprehend it. 'There is *something*,' she whispered. 'I can't quite grasp it.'

'Believe me,' said Lorna, 'when you've tasted a fresh kill, anything else is false. We were meant to hunt, you and I. I know it. Even Ratel was a hunter in the woods. We were meant to look after ourselves.'

'It's good to have him here,' Ellen said dreamily. 'Just like it used to be.'

'No. It can never be like that again,' Lorna answered exasperatedly. 'We have to escape. You will need all your strength. You must be as strong as me again.'

Ellen's health improved steadily. She ate almost as well as Lorna. Annie was ecstatic. She still visited the pen. She loved to see the sisters together. Lorna ignored her but Ellen occasionally came to the fence to rub her head against it when Annie was there. That was more than enough for Annie. She knew that Lorna's presence was the most important thing in Ellen's life now.

'Now you're not sad,' she would cry. 'Now you're happy!'

Photos were taken of the sister lionesses and articles written about their separation: what it had done to them, and how joyful their lives were now that they were together again. The honey badger was featured too for his part in the drama. But Joel was the hero of the hour who had devoted himself to reuniting the lionesses he had known since their cub days. He was interviewed by the press and television. No one asked him, now that his mission was accomplished, what he would do next. No one appreciated, it seemed, that he had in effect made himself redundant.

Lorna could think of nothing but escape. Day after day she paced her African enclosure, staring out beyond it to the savannah landscape. She and Ellen would walk separate paths, then meet, nuzzle each other and break apart again. Ellen was gradually putting on weight and Lorna constantly looked for the slightest chance of regaining freedom. She watched the routine comings and goings of staff; of Joel; she watched the deliveries of food and water; the arrangements for cleaning the lionesses' pen. At night-time she and Ratel would often talk about escape. The honey badger was every bit as eager as his lioness friend to fend for himself again.

'They've got a whole pack of us well fenced in here,' the badger told Lorna sourly. 'On my other side there's a family of warthogs. It seems the mother was injured when she was pregnant and was brought here by some of the men to bear her young in this place. They're still here.'

'My sister tells me that before you came there was a cheetah in your pen,' Lorna said. 'Where has she gone?'

'Who knows? Where are any of us to go? I've tried tunnelling but there are barriers set just as deep here as there were in the old place.'

'Humans can make mistakes,' Lorna growled. 'They only need to make one with me and I'll be off.'

'Will your sister go with you?'

'Yes. She can't live on her own. She nearly died here before I arrived. But I'm worried her reactions might not be quick enough yet. She has a lot to learn.'

'And would you wait for her?' the honey badger asked.

Lorna didn't answer at once. Then she said, 'That might make the difference between freedom and . . .'

'Imprisonment?' the badger suggested.

'Yes. It's very difficult.' Lorna turned to look at her sleeping sister. 'I couldn't abandon her,' she said finally. 'She *would* die next time.'

'Perhaps she'll sharpen up when she's back to full health,' said the badger.

'Perhaps.'

'I've been talking to Ratel,' Lorna told her sister later.

'I can guess what about,' said Ellen. 'Escape. That's all you think of.'

'What else is there?'

'I don't know. We never used to think about such a thing.'

'Oh, sister, if I could only make you understand. Why don't you talk to Ratel? He could tell you things. You used to talk a lot to him.'

'Yes,' said Ellen. 'In the old place. He's different now. I have tried talking, but I seem to make him impatient.'

'It's not you. It's being cooped up here. He had a new life like me and it was taken away from him.'

Ellen sighed. Always the same thing. 'If we did escape, how would we make out? I'd be a liability, wouldn't I?'

'Of course not. I'll soon show you how to catch your food.'

'I'm not strong enough for that.'

'Not yet. But you will be. You've come a long way already. And strength isn't the only thing. You need speed. And above all, stealth.'

'Quite a tall order really,' said Ellen ironically, 'when you've been provided for all your life.'

'If I could do it . . .'

'You were always bolder, sister,' said Ellen. 'Could you make me bold?'

'Hunger would do that,' said Lorna.

The more Ellen thought about the prospect of having to hunt, dim though it seemed, the more unlikely it appeared. In health she had never known real hunger and she couldn't share her sister's strange enthusiasm for courting it. Was freedom so wonderful if it made you suffer? She found herself hoping that the humans would remain too clever for the impatient Lorna. It never crossed her mind that in the long term the humans shared the same ambition for the lionesses as Lorna did.

The men watched the animals closely. Joel wanted to stay on until it was time for their release, but he was only on the newspaper's payroll to the end of the month. That was just over a week away, so Simon Obagwe offered him open house. Joel was profoundly grateful. He had come this far and to miss out on the final drama would have been a great disappointment. Ellen was improving day by day. She ate heartily and gained energy. Lorna's temper, however, had reached a new low point. She was completely unpredictable and the men began to fear her. Even Joel never took a chance with her.

The honey badger took to staring through the link fence at dusk, trying to gauge Lorna's mood before he passed a remark. She had become so touchy. Yet the sisters were as affectionate together as ever. They repeatedly nuzzled or licked each other in greeting as they moved about the pen. When they slept they always lay down together, heads or paws touching. It was a heartwarming sight. By comparison the badger's solitude was all the more dreary. How he would have liked a companion of his own!

'They don't have much time for me now,' he complained to himself as he watched the lionesses. 'Oh, if I could only get out of here!'

Ellen heard his growl and looked up. 'It's Ratel,' she said without interest, and yawned.

Lorna took a few steps towards the wire. 'Any plans?' she murmured.

'Plenty; and no means of carrying them out!' snapped Ratel.

'No change then,' Lorna grunted and turned away.

The next day a small section of the fence around Ratel's enclosure was removed. The badger had been declared fit and healthy and it was accepted that he must be a competent hunter after his long spell in the English woodland. Access to the surrounding savannah was suddenly presented to him. As it was his habit to hide in the daytime, it was early evening before this astonishing fact was noticed. Ratel could hardly believe his eyes.

'They've slipped up here,' he chuckled to himself, 'and *I* can slip *through*.' He would never know that his exit from Kamenza was expected, nor that the collar that had been fitted around his neck would enable the humans to keep track of his movements around the game park.

The lionesses weren't aware of Ratel's disappearance for a while. Their attention, particularly Lorna's, had been drawn to a number of small live mammals that had suddenly been introduced into their pen. This was part of the programme at Kamenza, to monitor the sisters' readiness and ability to make a kill. The small prey animals were hares and there wasn't much doubt about Lorna's intentions towards them as soon as she saw them. Her golden eyes widened and her head swivelled from side to side as she tried to follow the creatures' dashes from one point to another. When one of the little animals came close, Lorna pressed herself flat to the dusty ground. She was motionless; a statue. Her eyes fixed unwaveringly on the hare, her huge powerful shoulder muscles bunched ready to launch her forward the instant the prey was within range. Ellen lolled against a tree, watching Lorna with scant interest. The hare nibbled some grass, but then sensed it was in danger and took off. Lorna sprang. She missed her target and the hare scooted to the far end of the enclosure, sending all the others into a panic. They ran blindly hither and thither. Lorna spun round this way and that in an effort to track them. One darted by Ellen, who simply stared at it curiously.

'Sister! Sister!' Lorna roared in disbelief. 'Are you really so lazy?'

Ellen failed to answer. She had no idea what was expected of her. Finally Lorna stunned a hare with an outstretched paw, bowling it over and immediately following up the blow with a pounce that crushed the animal. Her once wounded paw had been used to propel her forward, but she felt nothing. Lorna seized the hare in her jaws and carried it to Ellen, dropping it in front of her. Ellen sniffed at it but showed no interest.

'This is prey,' said Lorna, beginning to rip the carcass apart. 'We can catch the others too. Didn't you feel any urge to chase the one that ran past you?'

'No,' Ellen replied. She guessed her sister was disappointed in her. 'I – um – wasn't hungry.'

'Neither am I,' Lorna told her. 'But I want to keep in trim. When you're stronger we'll give your turn of speed a test. You've been inactive too long, sister. We'll make you into something like a hunting lion yet!'

──14──

Roots

The remaining hares soon became much more careful. They found places in the long grass to hide. They didn't move around as much, so that they didn't attract attention. Lorna devoted her time to hunting them. Now that she had something to occupy herself she was less aggressive towards the people at Kamenza. She even allowed Joel to replenish the meat in the enclosure without challenging his presence. She ate sparingly, leaving most of the food for Ellen. She preferred the satisfaction of supplying her own needs. But she wasn't often successful.

Lorna's attempts to involve Ellen in her hunting sprees were watched by Joel and his colleagues. Ellen began to show some appreciation of the stealth and speed required to catch a hare off guard. She didn't actively join in a hunt but she took care not to disturb her sister when she was creeping towards her prey. She would remain silent and watchful while Lorna slunk on her belly through the dry vegetation of the pen. If Lorna had driven a hare in her direction she sometimes whipped out a paw and tried to bring the animal down. But her skill was negligible. Her reactions were too slow. Gradually, however, she was learning about the need to co-operate. This was vitally important if the lionesses were to rely on one another when the time came to adapt to life on the plains. Ellen's progress, however small, was noted and welcomed.

Lorna was the first to discover the honey badger's absence. She called him one night as she had used to do when they thought of nothing but escape. Her insistent growls brought no response.

'Strange,' she mused. 'He's never failed before. Can he have died in his burrow?' The thought made her unhappy and she started a series of melancholy roars. Ellen came running to pacify her.

'What's the trouble, sister? Don't fret.'

'I think Ratel has died,' Lorna said. 'He used to enjoy a chance to talk. He hasn't come this time.'

'Hasn't it occurred to you,' asked Ellen, 'that perhaps he has' – and she whispered – 'escaped?'

'Escaped? But how? He told me it was impossible. Oh, if he *has* got out and we're still . . .' She broke off and growled angrily.

'Still what?'

'HERE!' roared Lorna. She loped to the far side of the pen and peered out through the final enclosing fence to the outside world in the slight hope of a glimpse of the honey badger. Naturally he was nowhere to be seen. Lorna called him. Her roars reached a climax. The refuge centre echoed them back until the whole complex seemed to rumble. Ellen joined her sister. The two lionesses stood shoulder to shoulder, gazing out over the African landscape. Ellen began to roar, low at first, then she opened her throat and gave full-blooded cries that even competed with Lorna's.

People, Joel and Simon included, came running to the front of the lions' enclosure. Annie trembled. She had her hands to her ears. The din was incredible. It was raw, wild, and expressed a deep and primitive longing. Instinct had taken command. The lionesses were manifesting the wild animal's innate hostility to captivity: the frustrations, the discomfort, the falsity of a life dictated by human will. Ellen had been caught up in it almost unconsciously. The sisters yearned for freedom. The pull of their ancient homeland had exerted its sway. Joel recognised the significance of the moment. He turned to Simon. Their glances met and they nodded quietly.

'It's time,' said Simon.

'Yes,' said Joel. 'They've found their roots.'

For a couple more days the lionesses were fed reduced rations while Lorna, with some help from her sister, polished off the remaining hares. Ellen's return to health put on a spurt. She had filled out and she had a new confidence in herself. There was an eagerness about her which was a delight to see. Joel eventually began to wonder if the sisters could somehow tell that they were on the verge of an exciting adventure. They were restless. They patrolled the enclosure together, pausing now and then to stare with proud faces at their keepers as though looking for an expected signal. Then, early one morning, it came. An unusual bustle in the Kamenza refuge had the lionesses darting impatiently from one side of the pen to the other. They roared repeatedly, urging the men to hurry; to hasten their release. In a matter of moments, everything was transformed. An exit from the enclosure suddenly appeared on the far side as a section of fence was drawn upward, and they heard the voice of their old keeper, Joel, calling them by name for the last time.

'Farewell, Lorna. Farewell, Ellen. Go now. Go home. Go home. Go! Go!'

From the veranda of her house Annie waved and waved. Together, always together, the lionesses bounded out of the opening and loped through the long grass until they were just a tawny blur in the distance. The savannah engulfed them, easily finding space for two more beasts amongst the myriad already competing for life in its vastness.

Later, in the brief African twilight, Ellen and Lorna lay under an acacia tree. They had eaten. Lorna had chased and killed an elderly gazelle. Ellen had begun the chase too but her stamina was inadequate as yet and she had dropped out. Their meal had been interrupted by a pack of hyenas who had circled them as they ate their kill. Eventually the lionesses had been driven away by the pack's determination and superior numbers. The sisters had been taught an early lesson about competition and when to give way. But there was much more to learn. Ellen lay staring in the direction of Kamenza and the security of its enclosures. Lorna, however, gazed across the limitless distance of the game park. Her eyes missed nothing. She watched the movements of the different game species that were now their neighbours, assessing them for strength, swiftness, rivalry, danger. She saw how one species reacted to another and she knew that she and her sister had to go cautiously and, for the most part, quietly before they were able to count themselves part of the great scheme. There were unknown fears to conquer as they battled for survival. There was anticipation too – a nerve-tingling, thrilling anticipation of the hunt and the triumph of speed and cunning.

'Are you awake, sister?' Lorna asked. 'The air is cooling. There are new scents everywhere.'

'Yes, I'm awake,' Ellen answered. 'I've been listening to all the strange cries. They're quite disturbing. Whatever can they be?'

'That's what we're going to find out,' said Lorna.